D0090397

Books by Phyllis Reynolds Naylor

Shiloh Books
Shiloh
Shiloh Season
Saving Shiloh

The Alice Books
Starting with Alice
Alice in Blunderland
Lovingly Alice
The Agony of Alice
Alice in Rapture, Sort of
Reluctantly Alice
All But Alice
Alice in April
Alice In-Between
Alice the Brave
Alice in Lace
Outrageously Alice
Achingly Alice
Alice on the Outside
The Grooming of Alice
Alice Alone
Simply Alice
Patiently Alice
Including Alice
Alice on Her Way
Alice in the Know
Dangerously Alice

The Bernie Magruder Books
*Bernie Magruder and the Case
    of the Big Stink*
*Bernie Magruder and the
    Disappearing Bodies*
*Bernie Magruder and the
    Haunted Hotel*
*Bernie Magruder and the
    Drive-thru Funeral Parlor*

*Bernie Magruder and the Bus
    Station Blowup*
*Bernie Magruder and the
    Pirate's Treasure*
*Bernie Magruder and the
    Parachute Peril*
*Bernie Magruder and the Bats
    in the Belfry*

The Cat Pack Books
The Grand Escape
The Healing of Texas Jake
Carlotta's Kittens
Polo's Mother

The York Trilogy
Shadows on the Wall
Faces in the Water
Footprints at the Window

The Witch Books
Witch's Sister
Witch Water
The Witch Herself
The Witch's Eye
Witch Weed
The Witch Returns

Picture Books
King of the Playground
The Boy with the Helium Head
*Old Sadie and the Christmas
    Bear*
Keeping a Christmas Secret
Ducks Disappearing
I Can't Take You Anywhere
Sweet Strawberries
Please DO Feed the Bears

Almost Alice

Books for Young Readers

Josie's Troubles
How Lazy Can You Get?
All Because I'm Older
Maudie in the Middle
One of the Third-Grade
    Thonkers
Roxie and the Hooligans

Books for Middle Readers

Walking Through the Dark
How I Came to Be a Writer
Eddie, Incorporated
The Solomon System
The Keeper
Beetles, Lightly Toasted
The Fear Place
Being Danny's Dog
Danny's Desert Rats
Walker's Crossing

Books for Older Readers

A String of Chances
Night Cry
The Dark of the Tunnel
The Year of the Gopher
Send No Blessings
Ice
Sang Spell
Jade Green
Blizzard's Wake

Almost Alice

PHYLLIS REYNOLDS NAYLOR

Atheneum Books for Young Readers
New York • London • Toronto • Sydney

Atheneum Books for Young Readers
An imprint of Simon & Schuster Children's Publishing Division
1230 Avenue of the Americas
New York, New York 10020
Book design by Ann Zeak
The text for this book is set in Berkeley Old Style.
Manufactured in the United States of America
First Edition
2 4 6 8 10 9 7 5 3 1
Library of Congress Cataloging-in-Publication Data
Naylor, Phyllis Reynolds.
Almost Alice / Phyllis Reynolds Naylor. — 1st ed.
p. cm.
Summary: In the second semester of her junior year of high
school, Alice gets back together with her old boyfriend Patrick,
gets a promotion on the student newspaper, and remains a
reliable, trusted friend.
ISBN-13: 978-0-689-87096-5
ISBN-10: 0-689-87096-5
[1. Friendship—Fiction. 2. High schools—Fiction. 3. Schools—
Fiction. 4. Identity—Fiction.] I. Title.
PZ7.N24Aln 2008
[Fic]—dc22
2007037457

To our granddaughter Tressa,
with love

Almost Alice

Contents

The Trouble with Sadie

It had to be in person, and they all had to be there.

Gwen was at a meeting over the lunch period, so I couldn't tell them then. I waited till we went to Starbucks after school before I made the announcement:

"Patrick asked me to the prom."

Two seconds of silence were followed by shrieks of disbelief and excitement:

"Five months in *advance*? *Patrick*?"

"You're *kidding* me!"

"*When?*"

"Yesterday." I was grinning uncontrollably and couldn't help myself. "He called. We talked."

"He called. You talked. What is this? Short-hand?" Gwen demanded. "Girl, we want *details*!"

"Wait! Hold it!" said Pamela. She jumped up, went to the counter, and bought a huge cup of whipped cream, then liberally doused each of our lattes to celebrate.

"Now *dish!*" she said.

"Well, I was just hanging out in my room, getting my stuff ready for school, when I heard the phone ring."

"He didn't call you on your cell?"

"I'm not sure he knows the number."

"I'd think he would have had it programmed in!"

"It's been *two years,*" I told them, working hard to defend him. Defend whatever there was between us, though I didn't know myself.

Liz rested her chin in her hands. When she looks at you through half-closed eyes, you realize just how long and thick her eyelashes are—longer than any girl's lashes have a right to be. "Oh, Alice, you and Patrick!" She sighed. "I *knew* you'd get back together. It's in the stars."

Gwen, the scientist, rolled her eyes. She was looking especially attractive, her hair in a new style of cornrows that made a geometric pattern on top of her head. The gold rings on one brown finger matched the design of her earrings, and she was definitely the most sophisticated-looking of the four of us. She was also the only one who had visited three colleges so far and who had even picked up scholarship forms.

"How long did you guys go together, anyway?" she asked.

"I guess it was about eighth grade that I really started liking him. The summer before eighth through the fall of ninth grade." I was embarrassed suddenly that I remembered this so precisely, as though it were always there at the front of my consciousness. "We actually met in sixth, but sixth-grade boyfriends aren't much to brag about."

"He did have his goofy side," Pamela agreed. "Remember that hot day at Mark's pool when you fell asleep on the picnic table? And Patrick placed two lemon halves on your breasts for a minute?"

"What?" Gwen shrieked.

"Yes, and when I woke up, everyone was grinning and no one would tell me what happened. And I couldn't figure out what those two little wet spots were on the front of my T-shirt. Like I was nursing or something!"

We yelped with laughter.

I continued. "And the year he gave me an heirloom bracelet for my birthday that turned out to be his mom's, because she didn't wear it anymore."

"I never heard that one," said Liz.

"And Mrs. Long had to call me and ask for it back," I said. We laughed some more. I wondered if I was being disloyal, telling all this. That was the old Patrick. The kid. That was then, and this was now.

"So what attracted you to him in the first place?" asked Gwen. "Besides the fact that he's a tall, smart, broad-shouldered redhead? I wasn't in on that early history."

"Well, he wasn't always as tall or broad-shouldered," I said. "I guess it's because he's the most motivated, focused, organized person I ever met. His dad's a diplomat, and they've lived in Japan, Germany, Spain. . . . In some ways, he's a man of the world."

"And then he falls for Penny, the jerk," said Pamela. "I'm glad *that's* over."

I saw three pair of eyes dart in my direction to see how I was taking that, then look away. Wondering if I'd cry myself sick again if things didn't work out this time with Patrick. I remembered Elizabeth's organizing a suicide watch when Patrick and I broke up, so that a friend called every quarter of an hour to see if I was okay. I tried not to smile.

"Well," I said flippantly, "a lot can happen in the next five months. You know how everything else comes before fun where Patrick is concerned. And I didn't say we were back together. I just said we were going to the prom."

"But this is *his* prom, and then you can invite him back for *yours*!" said Liz excitedly, since Patrick's in an accelerated program that gets him through high school in three years.

"Yeah, and with *two* prom nights to make out, you know what *that* means," said Pamela.

"Will you *stop*?" I said.

To some girls, a prom means you're a serious couple. To some, it's the main event of high school. To some, it's the biggest chance in your life, next to getting married, to show off. And to some girls, it means going all the way.

"Well, I'm glad for you," said Gwen. "But I hope we don't have to talk prom for the next five months."

"Promise," I said.

"Some couples were just meant to be," Pamela said. "Jill and Justin, for example. They've been going out forever."

"What about you and Tim?" I asked. Tim had taken her to the Snow Ball last fall. A really nice guy.

"Could be!" said Pamela.

"So are you going to ask him to the Sadie Hawkins Day dance?" asked Gwen.

"I already have," Pamela told us, and grinned. Then she turned serious again. "Patrick better come through this time, Alice. He owes you big time."

If my friends didn't quite know what to make of Patrick, neither did I. I'd always thought of him as special somehow, but . . . My first boyfriend? More than that. Patrick was someone with a future, and I didn't know if I was part of that or not. Or wanted to be.

But you can analyze a good thing to death, so I decided to take it at face value: He really, really liked me and couldn't think of anyone he'd rather take to the prom. *Now enjoy it,* I told myself.

Our house was a mess. Dad and Sylvia were having the place remodeled, with a new addition on the back. Their bedroom, the kitchen, and the dining room were sealed off with heavy vinyl sheets so that dust and cold wouldn't get through. Their bed had been taken apart and stood against one wall in the upstairs hallway. The rest of their furniture was pushed into Lester's old bedroom, where they were sleeping, and their clothes were piled all over the place in my room. Downstairs, the dining-room furniture had been moved into the living room along with the refrigerator and microwave, and the construction crew had fashioned a sink with hot and cold running water next to the fridge. We ate our meals on paper plates, sitting in the only available chairs, knees touching.

"Maybe it wasn't such a good idea to stay in the house during remodeling," Dad said that weekend when we didn't think we could swallow one more bite of *Healthy Choice* or *Lean Cuisine*.

"But think of all the money we're saving by not living in a hotel!" said Sylvia. "The foreman said that if we can put up with painters and carpenters doing the finishing touches, we might be able to move into the new addition by the middle of March."

Fortunately for us, the construction company had another contract for an expensive project starting April 1, and had doubled the workforce at our place to finish by then.

Dad was at the Melody Inn seven days a week, Sylvia was teaching, and I was at school, so we didn't have to listen to all the pounding.

Lester came over one night and took us out to dinner.

"Hey," I said over my crab cake, "why don't we move in with Lester for the duration?"

He gave me a look. "Don't even think it," he said. "I'm surviving on five hours of sleep a night while I finish my thesis."

"Oh, Les!" Sylvia said sympathetically.

"You need to get some exercise," Dad told him.

"I run to Starbucks and back," Les said.

"But . . . you're not seeing anyone at all?" I asked.

"Not much," said Les.

It was hard to imagine, but somehow I believed him. Les had made up his mind to graduate, and he was hitting the books.

"What about that girl you were going out with at Christmas?" I asked him.

"It's over," said Les.

"Already?" exclaimed Dad.

"Too high maintenance," Les told us. "All she wanted to do was party, and I can't afford the time. So I've sworn off women till after I graduate."

That was even more difficult to imagine, but I felt real sympathy for my twenty-four-year-old brother right then. I decided that somehow, sometime around Valentine's Day, I . . . or Liz and I . . . or Liz and Pamela and I . . . or Liz and Pam and Gwen and I were going to plan a surprise for Lester. I just didn't know what.

Patrick has called me twice since New Year's Day, when he invited me to the prom. He didn't call to chat, exactly. He either had something to tell me or a question to ask. You could say he's all business, but that wouldn't be true, because he has a good sense of humor and there's a gentleness that I like too. I just wish he were more accessible. He runs his life like a railroad—always busy, always going somewhere, *getting* somewhere.

But there was a lot more to think about during the second semester of my junior year. The SATs, for one. I decided that January would probably be my least hectic month, so I'd take the test on January 26, then take it again later if I bombed the first time. Getting my braces off was item number two. I also wanted to spend more time with our friend Molly Brennan, who's getting treated for leukemia, and to persuade Pamela, if possible, to audition for the spring musical, *Guys and Dolls*. I'd signed up for stage crew once again.

Tim Moss was doing a lot for Pamela's self-confidence. Pamela's pretty, she's got a good voice, and has a great body. But ever since her mom deserted the family a few years ago and ran off with a boyfriend, Pamela's self-esteem has been down in her socks. Lately, though, now that her mom's back and living in an apartment alone, Pamela's seemed a little more like her old self, and once she started going out with Tim, she really perked up.

Sylvia, my stepmom, said that one way to tell

if a guy is right for you is if he wants what's best for you, encourages your talents, and—at the same time—has a good sense of self and where *his* life is going. She was speaking about my dad and her decision to marry him when she said that, but I think Tim Moss would just about get an A on all three.

"Go for it," Tim told Pamela when we were talking about the musical the other night.

"I'll think about it" was all she said, which is one step up from "No, I'd never make it," which is where she was last week.

And speaking of Sylvia, I'm getting along better with her. Even Annabelle, her cat. *Our* cat. The cat I'd said such awful things about last year. Sylvia and I are both trying to communicate more. If she wants my help with some big household project, for example, she doesn't descend on me some weekend when I have a ton of homework or something else planned. And if I want to use her or Dad's car, I try to remember to tell them in advance, not just spring it on them.

I guess you could say that for me and my friends, cars and driving are a big part of our lives. They were sure a big part of Brian Brewster's, whose license was just suspended last week in court because he hit another car in December and badly injured a seven-year-old girl. She was

in the hospital for three weeks with a broken pelvis and other injuries, but I think Brian would
have to break his own pelvis before he'd worry
more about her than about the fact that he can't
drive for a year.

I don't hang around much anymore with
Brian and his crowd. Patrick seems able to move
in and out of a crowd whenever the spirit moves
him; if there's one thing Patrick Long is not, it's
a label. But mostly I go places with Pamela, Liz,
and Gwen.

The four of us have different interests much
of the time, but we still tell each other a lot of personal stuff. Liz and I used to go running together
on summer mornings and sometimes after school.
But I wasn't fast enough for her, so she joined the
girls' track team this semester. Pamela was taking
voice lessons; Gwen got a job as a receptionist in
a clinic twice a week after school; and I promised
my friend Lori that I'd join the Gay/Straight Alliance at school to show my solidarity with her and
her girlfriend, Leslie.

But there was one secret I hadn't told anyone:
I had a crush on Scott Lynch, a senior, the editor in chief of *The Edge*. Last fall I'd done everything but beg him to take me to the Snow Ball,
but he'd asked a girl from Holton-Arms. So when
another senior, Tony Osler, asked me, I'd gone

with him. And because Tony seemed more interested in getting into my pants than anything else,
that didn't last very long. Now I was going to the
prom in May with Patrick and was wildly excited
about it, but Scott was still on my mind. Is life
ever simple?

I have to say that Jacki Severn, features editor for
The Edge, is not my favorite person. She's got an eye
for copy layout and she's a good writer, but she isn't
easy to work with. When I got to the staff meeting
on Wednesday, she was on one of her rants.

"I think we ought to change the name!" she
was saying. "It's historically inaccurate."

Now what? I wondered, exchanging glances
with Don Spiro, one of our photographers. *Hissy
fit,* he scribbled on a piece of paper and shoved it
across the table.

"What's up?" I asked the others.

Scott was balancing a pencil between two fingers and offered an explanation: "Remember that
last year the school decided to replace the Jack of
Hearts dance in February with something more
casual?"

I nodded. "Something fun and silly and
utterly retro, like a Sadie Hawkins Day dance."

"Right. Well, the dance committee has scheduled it for February twenty-ninth, because the

twenty-ninth happens only once every four years, sort of a nice kickoff for the first Sadie Hawkins Day dance. But Jacki wants to call it the 'Turnaround Dance.'"

I gave Jacki a puzzled look. "And if we call it 'Sadie Hawkins,' the world will end?" I asked, making Scott smile.

But Jacki sure didn't. "I've researched it, and Sadie Hawkins Day first appeared in a *Li'l Abner* comic strip in November 1937. If the whole rest of the country celebrates Sadie Hawkins Day in November, it's ludicrous to hold our dance in February unless we change the name."

"I doubt that the whole rest of the country even knows who Sadie Hawkins is," said Don.

"It doesn't matter!" said Jacki. "Besides, there's another SAT scheduled for March first, the day after."

"But not at our school," said Miss Ames, our sponsor. "And the newspaper has no authority to change the name of the dance. 'Sadie Hawkins' still lets people know that it's girls' choice."

"But—," Jacki began.

I was sitting at one of the computers and had Googled the term *Sadie Hawkins Day*. "Hey!" I interrupted. "Here's a West Virginia school that holds a Sadie Hawkins Day dance every February twenty-ninth."

Scott jokingly banged his notebook down on the tabletop. "Sold!" he said. "Next topic . . ."

Jacki gave me a long, hard look and angrily picked up her pen.

The topic may have been closed, but it sort of sealed the antagonism between Jacki and me. I guess I never quite forgave her for trying to do a story on Molly and her leukemia without any thought as to how Molly might feel about it. And Jacki probably never forgave me for being there with some of my friends, sitting on Molly's bed and eating a pizza with her—Molly in makeup, to be exact—when the photographer arrived to take a picture of a pale, limp girl in a lonely bed. Not exactly the story Jacki had in mind.

When I got home that night, I waited until I'd finished my homework before calling Patrick. I've always had the feeling he's out most evenings, because—in addition to his accelerated curriculum with all the extra homework—he's got band and track and probably other activities I don't even know about.

The phone rang three times before he answered.

"Hey!" he said.

"Hey, it's me. You busy?"

"Always, but I need a break. What's happening?" His voice was welcoming. Encouraging.

"We had a staff meeting after school—the newspaper," I explained, "and the big discussion was what to call the dance that's replacing the Jack of Hearts on February twenty-ninth."

"Pretty momentous. Right up there with the Mideast," said Patrick. Patrick always thinks global.

"Yeah. Jacki Severn's bummed because she says that most places celebrate Sadie Hawkins Day in November, so she wants to change the name of the dance."

Patrick laughed. "A slugfest between the Sadies and the non-Sadies? Glad I won't be there."

I was quiet for a moment. "Where will you be?"

"The band's quintet is playing for a big Kiwanis Club charity dance. They hold it every leap year on February twenty-ninth, and Mr. Levinson asked us two months ago to play."

"So . . . you won't be able to go?" I said, sounding stupid.

"Unless I've got a clone," said Patrick. And then he must have sensed what I was thinking, because he said, "You don't have to sit at home, Alice. You could invite someone else."

I guess I didn't want to hear that, either. I wanted him to sound disappointed. Jealous, even, at the thought of me in someone else's arms.

But Patrick went on. "I don't want you to feel that because we're going to the prom, I've got a clamp on your social life." Now he sounded like a sociology professor. "I mean, I'm going to be away next year."

"I know," I said, feeling a heaviness in my chest.

"So I don't want you sitting around waiting for me."

When somebody tells you he doesn't want you sitting around waiting for him, it means he won't be sitting around in Chicago waiting for you. And maybe I wanted to hear that, maybe I didn't.

"Well," I said. "I just . . . wanted to make sure. You were my first choice."

"That's good to know," said Patrick, a chuckle in his voice, and I could just imagine his eyes laughing then. "I'll think of you at the Kiwanis Club that night."

I asked him what instruments made up the quintet, and he said a clarinet, a bass, a trumpet, a sax, and drums—the drummer, of course, being Patrick. But I didn't really care. I was thinking, *Sadie Hawkins*; I was thinking, *Girls' Choice*; I was thinking, *Scott Lynch*.

2

Making the Call

I knew I shouldn't wait. If I was going to invite Scott, I had to do it now. My guess was that he had already been asked. How could he *not* have been asked—Scott, with the topaz blue eyes and the squarest chin I've ever seen; the tall, slim guy—taller than Patrick, even— with that special Scott smile for everyone, not just me.

My heart began to pound, and I wiped my palms on my jeans. Maybe he hadn't been asked. The dance committee had only recently settled on the date. I think Jacki Severn likes him too, but after she was shooting daggers at everyone at the staff meeting, Scott included, I doubted he was her date.

I stood up and went to the bathroom, then made my way back through the disassembled furniture in the hallway and sat down again on my bed. I stared at my cell phone. It was the scariest thing around.

What if he just put me off? That was almost more frightening than if he said no. What if he said, *You're kidding, right?* Then I'd have to say, *Uh . . . no, I really mean it. Do you want to go?* And he'd say, *Alice, I'm sorry, but you're just not my type.*

I let out my breath and went over to the window, feeling perspiration trickling down from my armpits. How do guys stand this? How do they get up in the morning wanting to ask a girl out, then watch the minutes tick by all day, knowing that every hour they wait, the girl is that much closer to going with someone else?

The phone in the hallway rang, and I jumped. Maybe Scott was calling me! Maybe he was calling to say that if I was thinking of inviting him to the Sadie Hawkins Day dance, please don't embarrass myself.

It was Lester.

"Did I leave my scarf there when I came by the other night?" he asked.

"Oh, you scared me!" I said. "I thought you were somebody else."

"I sound different?"

"No. But listen, Lester, if a girl asked you out and you didn't want to go, how would you tell her?"

"What does this have to do with my scarf?" he said.

"Nothing. But I won't look for your scarf unless you tell me what to expect."

I heard him sigh. "Who are you asking out? What's the matter with Patrick?"

"He can't go to the Sadie Hawkins Day dance because his quintet is playing for a Kiwanis thing, and I want to ask somebody else, but I'm positive he'll turn me down."

"Well, if you're positive, then save yourself the trouble," said Les.

"You're not helping!" I bleated. "I want to ask Scott Lynch, and I don't know how he really feels about me. He's nice to everyone."

"Then he'll be nice to you, even if he turns you down," said Lester.

"But tell me how *you'd* do it," I said. "I want to be prepared. How do guys do it without hurting a girl's feelings? I don't want to hang up not knowing whether he said yes or no."

"It's impossible to do it without hurting somebody. It *always* hurts to be turned down," said Lester. "But if I had to say no to someone and didn't have a good excuse, I'd make up something."

"You'd lie?" I said.

"Yeah," said Lester. "Now, about my scarf . . ."

"But what if you wanted to make sure she never asked you again? What do guys say *then*?" I insisted.

"I suppose they could say, 'I'm not that into you,' but I'd probably say, 'I'm flattered, but I just don't think it would work out for us.'"

"*Oof,*" I said, feeling sick already. "I don't think I can take this, Les. What would I *do* if he says something like that?"

"I guess you could sue him for mental anguish, but it wouldn't make him like you any better," said Lester. "Hey, Al, where's your spunk? I thought you were braver than this."

"I'm not," I told him. "I'm terrified. And every minute I don't call him, some other girl probably will."

"Okay, then. Call the guy! But before you do, have you seen my scarf?"

"Is it cashmere? Extra long? Sort of creamy beige?"

"Yes. Exactly."

"It's in my locker."

"What?" he yelped. "That was a gift from Lauren."

"Lauren!" I exclaimed. "Les, you broke up with her two years ago."

"So I can't wear her scarf? I *like* that scarf. Why is it in your locker?"

"You left it here, and I thought I'd wear it to school the next time I drove Dad's car, then deliver it to your apartment afterward. But I forgot and left it in my locker."

"I want it back, Al. They're predicting snow for tomorrow."

"I'll *bring* it, Les! Calm down! I didn't lose it or anything," I told him.

After I went back in the bedroom, I picked up my cell phone and punched in Scott's number. A woman answered on the second ring.

No! No! What was his mom doing on his cell phone? Then I realized I'd dialed the second number I'd scribbled in my staff notebook, his home number.

"I . . . I wonder if I could speak to Scott?" I said, wanting to die. I know you're supposed to identify yourself when you call, but I didn't want her announcing it.

"I'm sorry, but he's not in right now, and I see he left his cell phone here. I expect him back in twenty minutes, though," she said. "Should I have him call you?"

The phone felt clammy in my hand. I had to go through this a second time?

"Uh . . . no, that's okay. I'll call back," I told her, and went to the bathroom again. *Geez!* Why hadn't I just told Scott's mom to ask him to the dance for me? Then, when he said no, I wouldn't have to hear it from him.

Why are boyfriends' mothers so scary? I wondered. Mrs. Long always sounded so elegant and polite that I usually used the wrong words. Sam's mom was positively terrifying. Scott's mom sounded okay, but how did I know what she'd tell him?

Forty minutes later, though, at 9:50, I called his cell phone number.

"Hi, Alice," he said.

I was afraid I would faint. "H-how did you know it was me?" I asked.

"Um . . . caller ID?" he said, and I could almost see him smiling.

"Oh. Right," I said. "Hope I didn't interrupt anything."

"No. I just got back from the gas station. What's up?"

"About the Sadie Hawkins Day dance . . . ," I began.

"Not you too!" he said.

I was stunned. What? A dozen girls had called so far?

Then he said, "You want to change the name?"

"No!" I said. "Actually, I'm calling to see if you'd like to go with me."

Was it one second before he answered? Three? Five? "To the dance? Uh . . . sure," he said. "Sounds like fun! Thanks."

I was speechless.

"Alice?" he said.

"Oh, that's great!" I told him. "Great! I'll buy the tickets and everything."

"Okay. We can figure all that out later," said Scott.

"Great!" I said again. Was that my third *great*? "Okay, then, I'll see you at school tomorrow."

"Right," said Scott. "G'night."

"'Night," I said, and I think I actually wet my pants a little.

The first person I told was Liz, and I wished I hadn't. Wished I'd told her at a different time, maybe, or in a different way, and with less emotion.

Elizabeth Price is gorgeous. Of the four of us—Pamela, Liz, Gwen, and me—I think she's the beautiful one. Long dark hair, dark eyes, creamy skin. . . . But it's funny about Liz. She *must* know she's gorgeous, but she doesn't act as though she knows. In fact, Liz is definitely on the shy side.

She had a serious boyfriend, Ross, from the summer before last when we were counselors at a kids' camp. They got together a few times after that, but Ross lives in Pennsylvania and we live in

Maryland. It was just too hard, I guess, to keep a long-distance romance going. But she hasn't been out with anyone since, and she absolutely refuses to let us set her up with anyone.

One of the problems is that a lot of guys mistake her shyness as being stuck-up or something. They figure a girl as beautiful as Liz must have a dozen guys calling her every weekend. Little do they know that Liz would love to go out, but no one asks her.

So when I called and breathlessly told her that Scott Lynch—our senior newspaper editor, a great-looking guy everyone notices when he walks down the hall—would be my date for the Sadie Hawkins Day dance, I didn't get the squeal I thought would follow.

"You're going with someone else? Not Patrick?" she asked.

I explained where Patrick would be that night and how I'd secretly been crushing on Scott. But she still didn't sound too excited. "Well, gosh, Alice! You're doing okay," she said, and somehow her voice sounded flat. "*Two* guys."

And then I felt awful.

"Why don't you come with us?" I said. "*Ask* somebody."

"Oh, sure. I'll just pick a name out of the student directory," she said.

"No, but there must be *some* guy you've got your eye on, Liz. I was amazed that no one had asked Scott yet, so other guys must still be available."

"Well, I can make that decision myself," Liz said, and I couldn't believe that this was Elizabeth Price, one of my best friends since sixth grade, sounding envious of me.

"Liz, are you mad or something?" I asked.

"Why should I be mad?"

"I don't know, but you don't sound like yourself," I said, feeling more uncomfortable by the second.

"I just don't need a cheerleader for my social life," she said.

"Liz, I—!"

"Anyway, I've got stuff to do," she said. "I'll see you tomorrow, okay?"

"*Not* okay!" I said. "If I said anything to upset you, Liz, I'm sorry!"

"I *said* I'm not upset."

"All right," I said, and we hung up.

I sat there staring out the window at the big white house across the street, wondering if she was over there looking out at me. Why did I think everyone should be as excited and happy for me as I was for myself? They'd already cooed and carried on when I said that Patrick had asked me to the prom, and now, a few weeks later, did I expect them to turn cartwheels because I had a second guy? It even surprised *me*. Yet, just because we were best friends, couldn't I understand that Liz might be a little jealous? *Tired* of me, even?

I have to say, I handled it pretty well the next day. I really tried to put myself in Elizabeth's place. If *I* hadn't gone out with a guy for a long time, and a friend called to tell me she had dates with *two* guys, and then apologized for upsetting me, how would I want her to treat me the next day?

I decided that another apology would only emphasize the fact that she didn't have a boyfriend. So I didn't even mention our phone conversation. She happened to be wearing a yellow sweater, and with her dark hair and lashes, she looked terrific.

"That's a great color on you," I said as I hung up my jacket in my locker.

"Thanks," she said.

At lunch I didn't mention the Sadie Hawkins Day dance. I think Liz was surprised that I talked about our cat instead, how she kept forgetting where her litter box was among all the stuff piled in our living room.

Someone eventually brought up the dance,

and when I still didn't bite, Liz said, "Hey, did you know that Alice invited Scott Lynch?" and everyone turned toward me.

I casually explained that he was a friend from the newspaper staff, that I'd asked him because Patrick was busy that night.

"Well, hey!" said Pamela.

"Wow!" said Gwen.

But I was so offhand about it that the attention soon shifted to someone else. And when Liz asked me later if I had a tampon, I gave her the only one I had left. What are friends for?

I was nervous about seeing Scott at school. I mean, one day we're friends working on the newspaper together, and the next we've got a date for a dance. Did he realize I'd had a crush on him for a long time, or did he think it was just a spur-of-the-moment invitation? All the way to school that morning, I'd mentally practiced what I'd say if I met him in the hall. Had even stood in front of the mirror practicing a smile that wasn't too eager, not too strained, not too wide, not too narrow. . . . I was making myself sick.

And then, just before gym, I was putting some stuff in my locker when I heard a voice say, "Hi, Alice," and there was Scott, books tucked under one arm.

"Oh!" I tried to speak and swallow at the same time, and started coughing. He grinned and patted me on the back.

"You okay?" he asked, and I felt my face growing hot.

"Yeah," I said, trying to laugh it off. "I didn't know you were there."

"Sorry!" he said, and waited till the coughing was under control. "Well, look. About the dance . . ."

He's backing out! I thought, feeling weak in the knees.

". . . I don't want to disrupt your plans or anything, but Don e-mailed me last night and said a girl had invited him, and he wanted to know if we could double. I know that this is your party, but I was going to offer to drive and . . ."

I was so relieved, I almost choked again. "Of course! It's fine!" I said.

Don was the senior photographer for our newspaper, and he and Tony had been with Liz and me last semester when I'd researched my feature story "The City at Night." Don's a nice guy. Then I had another thought: What if the girl who had invited him was Jacki Severn? What if we were double-dating with Don and Jacki?

"Is Don taking anyone I know?" I asked.

"Another senior, Christy Levin," he said.

I smiled. "Great," I said. This was great. Scott was great. Life was great.

"I'll tell him, then," Scott said, and nodded down the corridor. "Gotta run. Chem's at the other end of the building."

"See you," I called out.

Pamela was out with Tim Moss on Saturday night, so Gwen and Liz and I went to Molly's to play Scrabble with her.

She wasn't wearing her old sweat suit this time, but had on jeans and a fleece pullover, a baseball cap on her head.

"You look like you're feeling better," I told her, and she did.

"It's been an okay week," she told us. "Either the chemo's helping or I'm just getting more used to it."

She had the board set up on a card table in one corner of the family room, and her mom brought in a high-calorie shake for her, Cokes and chips for the rest of us.

Q, of course, is the most difficult letter to play because you need a U to go along with it. All the tiles were drawn, and I got stuck with a Q at the end of the game, while Molly was stuck with two U's.

"Two!" I cried. "You've been holding out on me, Molly!"

But in the next game Molly played the word *quiz*, with the high-scoring Q *and* the Z.

"Whoeee!" she cried, and even her dad looked in and grinned.

"Hey, girl, you've got those tiles marked!" Gwen joked.

Molly held up the two letters to show that the backs of the tiles were clean. "X-ray vision," she said. "I can see through wood."

I wished I could see through things. Through people. I wished I could see through Molly and tell if the treatment protocol she was on was working. I wished I could read the fortunes of all four of us there at the card table: Molly, the sickest of the lot; Gwen, the smartest; Liz, the most beautiful; and me, the most ordinary. It would be interesting to know what each of us would be doing three years from now. Five years. Ten years. . . .

Then again, maybe not.

3

Yo Te Quiero

The SAT wasn't as bad as I'd expected. Maybe, having taken the PSAT last fall, I was better prepared or wasn't as nervous. I can't say I sailed through it, but I felt more confident than I had before. I'd been boning up on it every week since October and attended two Saturday workshops in January, and that helped. Liz took the test with me, and we both were relieved and hopeful when it was over. At last we could think about other things for a while.

Liz was really into track, but the school newspaper kept me busy, and I wanted to get back to working for Dad at the Melody Inn on Saturdays, to earn some cash. Then there was the Gay/Straight Alliance, and on the first Thursday in February, I went to my first meeting.

It was good to know that Lori thought enough of me to invite me into the group and nice to see how much in love she and Leslie were with each other. The GSA had only been active in our school since last fall, though there were chapters in lots of high schools and colleges all over the country—just straight and gay friends, bonding together, offering support, so that gays didn't have to feel like a separate species and straights didn't have to feel they'd be labeled if they stood up for gay rights.

Everyone was sitting around in a loose circle when I came in, kidding with each other, sharing iPods, discussing new bands, showing off new jackets or hairstyles. I slid onto a chair next to Lori and listened to the chatter. Finally Mr. Morrison, the faculty sponsor, came in, said hello to the group, welcomed the new people, then started some sort of casual ritual, which everyone seemed to understand except me.

"My name is James," he said, smiling around the room, "and my socks are blue."

Whaaaaat? I thought. What did that have to do with anything? Especially because, glancing at his feet, I saw that his socks were definitely *not* blue, they were brown. Everyone was smiling, and I could tell that a lot of people were watching me, the new kid, to see *my* reaction.

Mr. Morrison turned to the person next to him, a large guy, one of the football players maybe, and this guy continued the ritual: "My name is Cary, and my socks are red."

His socks were *white*! What was going on? Were we talking in code or something? How did you play this game?

A girl was next. She grinned. "I'm Denisha, and my socks are pink." Yeah, they were. Well, coral maybe. It was hopeless.

As the strange ceremony continued, Lori leaned over and whispered, "The socks under your *pants*." And when I stared at her quizzically, she whispered, "Your underwear. But Morrison won't let us say that in case some parent goes berserk and tries to shut the group down."

What? Then it was Leslie's turn, then Lori's: "My name is Lori, and my socks are white."

What color underwear did I put on this morning? I thought desperately. But it was my turn, and all eyes were on me. All faces smiling.

"My name is Alice," I said, "and my socks are . . . are polka dot."

Everybody broke into laughter, and I was in. And I understood what the ritual was all about. In a way, it was a takeoff on Alcoholics Anonymous, where each person gives his first name and admits that he's an alcoholic. He says the words to own it—to make sure he recognizes that this is his problem.

But here, by describing our underwear, we were saying in effect that what we were didn't matter. We all wear underwear—well, except for one guy who said he wasn't wearing any socks at all. But who cared if they were red or blue? Who cared if you didn't *know*? Nobody had to answer that he or she was gay or straight or bisexual or transsexual because it wasn't considered a problem.

The next half hour was a sort of free-for-all. Anyone could share something that had happened during the past week—any problems, feelings, whatever.

"Somebody asked me how I felt about the word 'queer,'" one boy said. "And I thought, 'I don't know, man.' It seems okay when my friends and I use it, but if someone else calls me that . . . I'm not sure."

"Doesn't bother me," said another guy. "I look at it as a sort of status thing. You know, *Queer Eye for the Straight Guy*. Like we're the ones with style."

Somebody told a derogatory joke he'd heard in the locker room, and we talked about that for a while. This drifted into a joke-telling session, till we were so far off course that Mr. Morrison had to drag us back to business.

"We were planning to have a table at the

Sadie Hawkins Day dance," he said. "Everybody okay with that?"

"No one expects trouble, do they?" asked Leslie.

"There wasn't any trouble at the Snow Ball, and there were at least three gay couples there," someone answered.

"Whose turn is it to table?" Morrison asked.

"Phil's and Lori's," said someone, checking a clipboard, and for the rest of the session there was a recap of coming events and distribution of new brochures describing GSA, and then the meeting was over and everyone left.

I felt pretty good as I drove home in Sylvia's car. I think that the more groups you join, the more you feel you belong. And to tell the truth, I felt very content at that moment—two guys, three best friends plus a bunch of others, a dad and a brother whom I loved, a stepmom I was beginning to love. . . .

And then, as always, I felt the wave of sadness that my real mom wasn't alive for me to talk with—that the last time she'd seen me, I was five years old. I wished she could have known me now.

It was time to do something for Lester. I asked Gwen and Liz and Pamela if they'd help me decorate his car for Valentine's Day to make him think he had a secret admirer. Then he wouldn't wonder if he was losing his appeal, and he could concentrate more on his studies and finish his master's thesis. Not that he *was* wondering, but then, people are always insecure after a breakup, aren't they? And hadn't he just broken up with the "party girl"?

Valentine's Day was on a Thursday. Gwen, Pamela, and Liz agreed to go with me around nine on Wednesday evening to lavishly decorate his car. Yolanda, Gwen's friend from church, wanted to go with us, so that made five. I just said I was going out with my gal pals, and Dad let me have his car. I told him I'd be back around ten.

We had ribbons and streamers and hearts and paper bouquets. We had valentine messages printed on hearts. We whooped and giggled all the way down Georgia Avenue and made the turnoff at last into Takoma Park.

Lester lives in the upstairs apartment of a big Victorian house owned by Otto Watts, who's elderly and lives in the rooms down-stairs. Les has two roommates, Paul Sorenson and George Palamas, and our big worry was that one of them might come home late and catch us in the act. But when I pulled up in front of the house next door, we saw two cars in Mr. Watts's driveway and Lester's car parked at the curb.

"Are we lucky or are we lucky?" I whispered as we got out; we didn't even close the car doors, we were that quiet. Just reached in and took out all the stuff we'd prepared at home.

"Gwen, why don't you and Pamela and Yolanda do the rear windshield, and Liz and I will do the front," I suggested. "Then we'll drape streamers along both sides and take off."

Liz and I taped love messages against the front windshield so that the words could be read from the driver's seat. *Your secret crush*, read one. *Loving you from afar*, read another. There were bows and arrows, *X*'s and *O*'s, and *I love you* in three different languages.

We taped a large pair of open lips on a side window, cardboard "eyes" with fringed eyelashes over each headlight, a plastic cupid where a hood ornament might have gone. We tied a pair of black lace panties to the antenna.

Then the five of us unfurled the red and pink and white crepe paper streamers along each side of the car and around the bumpers. When I reached the door handle, I started to wrap the streamer twice around it to keep it from dragging, when suddenly the car erupted into a series of loud honks and beeps and sirens.

I jumped backward.

A theft alarm! When had Lester installed *that*?

"Omigod!" cried Pamela.

"Run!" I yelled. "Hide!"

We grabbed the rest of the streamers and started to run. Gwen lost her shoe, and we stopped to retrieve that, then barreled on, collapsing behind a panel truck parked two houses down.

Porch lights came on. A door opened. Then another.

"Alice, why didn't you *tell* us it was wired?" Gwen breathed on the back of my neck as we crouched practically on top of each other.

"It wasn't before! I didn't know!" I cried.

"They went that way!" a woman hollered. "I saw them running. I bet they're after the air bags!"

"Whose car is it?" we heard a man yell.

And another answered, "That one in front. Looks like somebody just got married."

I didn't realize anyone paid attention to those burglar alarms anymore. They're always going off, and nobody gets too excited. If we'd only had a minute longer . . .

We heard footsteps coming down the steps at the side of the house, and I knew in my bones it was someone from Lester's apartment.

"What the . . . ?" came a familiar voice.

A pause, then laughter.

"Hey, Les, somebody's got *your* number," another voice said.

The beeping stopped, and there was a long, plaintive yell from Lester: "Al-lice!"

"How did he know it was *me*?" I whispered to the other girls. "How? *How?*"

"Your dad's car," said Liz, and I crumpled.

"Al!" Lester bellowed again.

"Come on," said Gwen. "We've got to face the music."

Slowly we came out from behind the panel truck and walked sheepishly back toward Les and his two roommates, streamers trailing behind us. George Palamas, the shorter, dark-haired guy, was laughing, and Paul Sorenson was trying to read the messages on the rear window.

"That's them!" shouted the woman across the street on the front steps.

And at that very moment a squad car came rolling down the street, its light flashing.

"Al-lice!" Liz cried shakily.

The police car pulled over, and two officers got out.

"It's okay," called Les. "We've got 'em."

The policemen didn't respond, just came walking over, hands touching their belts. What they saw, of course, was three grown men with five young girls, and Les had his hand tightly on the back of my neck.

"Who called?" asked one officer.

"That's them!" screeched the woman across the street. "I saw 'em running."

"They were hiding behind that panel truck," yelled someone else.

"Oh, brother!" said George.

"So what's the problem here?" asked the second officer. And to Les, he said, "Put your hands down, please."

Les instantly released his grip on my neck.

"We didn't really do anything," I said quickly. "I'm his sister."

"We all did it together!" cried Liz.

"*Jeez!*" Les said through clenched teeth.

"The car!" Gwen said quickly, the only one of us who sounded intelligent just then. "All we did was decorate his car."

The policemen looked from us to the car and back again.

"Someone reported that there was an attempted car theft," said the first officer. "That didn't happen?"

"My sister here set off my car alarm, and someone must have seen them running," Les explained. "The neighborhood's had some air bags stolen recently, and we're sort of looking out for each other, that's all."

"We didn't take anything, honestly!" I said.

One of the officers gave us a weary smile, then turned to Les again. "You want the girls to undecorate your car?" he asked.

"Not until you've read the messages!" said Pamela. "We worked hard on this!"

"I'll handle it," Les told the policemen. "Thanks."

They got back in the cruiser and took off.

The people on their porches turned then and went back inside. Lester stared at his car, then at me. "Al—," he started.

But Pamela interrupted. "We're freezing, Lester. Can't we come in for something hot before we undecorate it?"

He sighed. "Come on," he said, and turned toward the steps.

Four of us squeezed together on the sofa, and Pamela sat on the floor, holding a coffee mug. Liz and Pam hadn't been in Lester's apartment since he'd let us help him move in, and Gwen and Yolanda hadn't seen it at all.

George sat across the room reading some of

the heart messages he'd torn off the back wind-shield. Paul was rummaging around the kitchen for another cup.

"What *is* all this, Al?" Les asked. "What were you trying to do?"

"Haven't you ever heard of Valentine's Day?" I asked.

"And you figured I needed a heart?"

"She just wanted you to feel loved, Lester," said Pamela, smirking.

"Like a secret admirer or something," put in Liz.

"To keep you happy so you could concentrate on your studies," said Gwen, trying not to laugh.

Les stared at the five of us like we had just sprouted feathers. "Are you insane?" he asked, directing the question to me. "You figured that if I thought there was a woman secretly in love with me, I'd go happily back to my thesis and forget about her? Al, if there was a hot babe watching me from the bushes, I'd be out there *looking* for her; I'd be prowling the sidewalks, patrolling the streets, checking out every coffee shop in a five-mile radius from the U. Are you nuts?"

I leaned back against the cushions. "I guess I am," I said.

George was still reading the love messages.

"*Io t'amo? Yo te quiero? Je vous aime?* Who wrote these?" he asked.

"*The Berlitz Phrase Book for Travelers,*" said Gwen, and that made us all laugh.

"So who's taken Spanish?" George asked.

"I have," said Yolanda and Liz both.

"And who wrote these?"

"I did," said Yolanda. "Well, sort of. My boyfriend did them for me."

"What's *Por favor, traigame otro tenedor*?" George asked, and I began to get the picture. George may be Greek or whatever, but he knew his Spanish.

"Uh . . . please . . . uh . . . ," Liz began.

"Please bring me another fork," said George. "What's *Tome izquierda despues del puente*?"

"Turn . . . ," Liz began again, then stopped.

"Turn left beyond the bridge. You girls flunk. Time to go home." He grinned.

The phone rang just then, and Mr. Watts, down below, wanted to know why that car out front was all dressed up like a birthday cake and whether the girls had brought over anything to eat. Les told him that no, unfortunately, no one was having a party, but Paul was going to get Chinese takeout on Friday, and Mr. Watts was invited.

Because Pamela had finally finished her tea,

we put on our jackets, apologized once more to Les, and promised to take the stuff off his car before we left. He said he'd also settle for a wash job and vacuuming come spring.

"You and your bright ideas," Gwen said to me as we pulled the last heart off the windshield.

"But we got to see the inside of their apartment, didn't we?" said Pamela. And that made it all worthwhile.

Our high school doesn't allow students to have flowers or candy sent to the school office for pickup on Valentine's Day. In fact, Valentine's Day had gotten out of hand, with some of the more popular girls carrying around armloads of stuffed animals and chocolates and roses and stuff, while others—most of us, in fact—got nothing.

So the rule was that any Valentine's Day gifts arriving at the front office would be delivered to the nursing home down the street and that any Valentine's Day gift given privately from one student to another had to be kept in the locker till the end of the day.

We missed the Jack of Hearts dance, now that it was crossed off the calendar, but we had Sadie Hawkins to look forward to. And I was thinking of Scott as I walked to my locker after the last class.

I turned the dial on my lock and opened the door. Someone must have given out my locker combination, because there on my rumpled gym clothes at the bottom lay a single white rose. And a card beside it read *Patrick.*

You know how you can feel thrilled and horrified at the same time? Justified and guilty? It was almost as though I were cheating on Patrick.

Oh no! I thought. I hadn't given him anything! Didn't think we were . . . well, a couple. Not yet, anyway. Had he found out I'd asked Scott to the dance? Is that what this was about? Or did the rose mean he really cared?

I had a right to go with Scott. I knew that. Hey, who was it who once told me he wanted to go out with both Penny and me? Plus, Patrick had actually suggested I go to this dance with someone else. What I was keeping from him, though, was how big a crush I had on Scott.

I stood there staring down at the flower. Who was it who wrote, *A rose is a rose is a rose . . .* ? No, it wasn't. It was a little white bundle of ambiguities, and I wondered just how this semester was going to play out.

4

Suggestions

Pamela and Tim were getting to be about as close as any couple in high school, except for Jill and Justin maybe, who had been going out forever. Tim was considerate of Pamela, patient with her, and Pamela, in turn, liked to think of little ways to please him. She carried Tylenol in her bag for him when he had a headache, bought a refill for his pen, saved her dill pickle for him at lunch. . . . They really seemed to care for each other, and it was nice to see Pamela so happy.

I wish she could have told her mom about him. I was just getting to the place where I could confide in Sylvia now and then, and I liked that. But Pamela and her mom still fought much of the time.

Of the four of us—Pamela, Elizabeth, Gwen, and I—Pam was the only one right then with a bona fide boyfriend. I had two dates for two dances, but I couldn't call either one a boyfriend. Gwen was too wrapped up in AP courses to go out much, and Liz *wanted* a guy, but it just wasn't happening, and it was Liz I was thinking about.

What do you say to a girlfriend to make her a little more flirtatious? A little more friendly? A little more sexy or fun or approachable or *some-* thing?

"It's your smile that turns guys on," I told her once.

"Joke around with the guys the way you do with us," Gwen said.

"When a guy follows you with his eyes, Liz, flirt *back*!" Pamela suggested.

We might as well have been trying to teach a cat to fly, I decided. Liz just didn't seem to have it in her. When the four of us were together, check-ing out a cute guy, or when we were around guys she *knew* were out of our league, she could play along. And obviously, when she and Ross fell for each other at camp two summers ago, she must have been more approachable then. In fact, I would have called her enthusiastic about guys. But when it came to boys at school, guys in our classes, guys who had *boy*friend potential, she shriveled up, like she didn't want to take the chance.

I think maybe part of the problem was that

Liz took her romances a little too seriously. Her first boyfriend was Tom Perona, the summer before seventh grade, but he dumped her for a new girl at his school.

She had a crush on a teacher at the beginning of eighth, but of course that went nowhere. Then she fell for Justin Collier—before he started going out with Jill—but once he made a remark about her weight, it was over. Then there was Ross, and he was about as perfect for her as we could imagine, but the long-distance thing just didn't work out, and she didn't want to get hurt again.

But now it was like she'd forgotten how to try. It made me tired sometimes. Between trying to get Liz to be more friendly, Gwen to lighten up on her studies, and Pam to try out for the spring musical, I felt that I was using a lot of energy on my friends. And it made me wonder if there were things about *me* they'd like to change.

When I went to work at my Dad's music store on Saturday—I run the little Gift Shoppe in the alcove under the stairs—David asked me if I'd had a good Valentine's Day. David Reilly is one of Dad's part-time employees. He's about twenty and is thinking of becoming a priest.

"Define 'good,'" I said.

He smiled. "Okay. Something from a boyfriend maybe?"

"I don't have a particular boyfriend," I said. "But I did get a white rose, and I bought myself some M&M's on the way home."

He laughed. "Oh, too bad. I was hoping you had a stash of chocolates somewhere."

A woman came in the store just then wanting to sign her child up for trumpet lessons, and David took her to meet the instructor on the upper level. When he came down, I realized I hadn't asked him how things went in New Hampshire over Christmas. He'd told me he wanted to talk over things with his parents and his girlfriend— decide which he wanted more: the church or a wife. So I asked.

David leaned against the display case where I was polishing the glass top and stared down at the trays of novelty items. He's a really good-looking guy. Dark hair, square jaw, great clothes, great voice. He also sings in a men's choir. "I wish I could say I came back with a clear answer," he said. "My folks said they'd accept whatever decision I made. My girlfriend's the only one who's definite. She said she needed a decision by summer, that she won't wait for me after that. She doesn't want a half commitment."

I couldn't say I blamed her. "Did you talk it over with a priest?" I asked.

"Many times," he said. "They don't want a halfhearted commitment either. 'Finish college,' they say. 'Then think about seminary. Take a few courses and see if you know yourself better by then.' But that's too long for Connie."

"What's she like?" I asked as I rearranged the silver earrings and the necklaces made out of eighth notes.

He smiled. "Pretty. An inch taller than I am, and probably smarter, too. We broke up once already. But I'm down here taking courses at Georgetown, she's up in New Hampshire—I don't know. I think the church is winning."

"How do you ever know for sure?" I asked.

"You don't. You don't know anything for sure, Alice. Some of us take a leap of faith into religion, into marriage, and hope for the best. Some people embrace uncertainty and don't have any problems with doubt. It all depends on what you can live by, what makes you a better person."

"I have a lot of doubts about a lot of things," I told him.

"So do I," said David. "And people handle them differently, that's all."

• • •

I didn't have a chance to thank Patrick for the rose until the following Monday, because he was at some kind of a three-day science competition in Baltimore. If ever a person had too many interests, it was Patrick, but I didn't mind being one of his interests.

What I wanted to know was just where I was on the list—high priority or low? How many other things were ahead of me? I wondered sometimes if Patrick had any idea how much he'd hurt me when he'd said if he had to choose between Penny and me, it would be Penny. How does a girl ever get over a comment like that? But if she holds a ninth-grade mistake against a guy all the way up through eleventh, how mature is *that*?

"Elizabeth's gone out for track this semester," I told him after I'd mentioned the rose and we'd talked a few minutes.

"Yeah. I saw her running a couple days ago after school. Some of the other guys on the team noticed her too," Patrick said.

"Well, I wish one of them would ask her out," I said.

"You mean Liz can't get a guy?" asked Patrick.

Are all males this clueless? I wondered.

"Nobody asks her, Patrick!" I said.

"Well, I guess she *is* a little scary," he said.

"What do you mean, scary? Elizabeth?"

"Sort of perfectionistic. I mean, she *looks* so perfect that I guess if I asked her out, I'd worry that everything would have to go just right."

"Uh . . . *have* you ever thought of asking her out? Just curious."

"Maybe once or twice."

"Why didn't you?" I teased.

"Told you. I might order a hamburger and find out she'd turned vegan. I might wear sneakers and she was expecting loafers with tassels or something."

I laughed. "Patrick, I can't ever imagine you worrying about details. In fact, I can't imagine you worrying much about anything at all."

"You don't know me, Alice," he said.

"Really? What do you worry about, other than grades?"

"Life," he said, and then he laughed a little too. "Sometime when you've got six hours, I'll fill you in."

When we were laying out the next issue of *The Edge*, I asked Don about Christy Levin. "Someone I should know?"

"Probably not, but you'll like her. She's on the girls' basketball team. Brunette, kind of tall. . . . I took her to the Snow Ball."

"I'll probably recognize her when I see her," I said.

Scott came over. "What time do you want me to pick you up on the twenty-ninth?"

"Seven would be fine," I told him.

The dance committee had their work cut out for them, getting students familiar with the famous Al Capp comic strip *Li'l Abner*, most popular in the forties and fifties. They made poster-size reproductions of some of the strips and hung them in the hallways. There was handsome Abner, who had no idea that the full-lipped Daisy Mae was pining for him; Mammy Yokum and her pipe; luscious Moonbeam McSwine, who slept with the pigs—all those crazy characters.

It was all so dorky, so different, that it seemed to be catching on. Kids stood together in the halls, reading the strips and laughing, and some of them began imitating the characters—scratching their armpits, walking in Mammy's bowlegged stride, adopting Abner's clueless expression. Each day there was a new strip, and we heard girls talking about what they were going to wear.

And of course this was just what the school wanted—an informal dance that everyone could afford to attend. It would be an all-evening event, including a Dogpatch barbecue. The ticket price covered everything, so the girls didn't have to

take the guys anywhere before the dance. No corsages. Just an evening in the high school gym.

I was getting excited now, and with Scott
doing the driving, that made it simple. Still, Scott
and Don and Christy were all seniors, and I wondered how I'd fit in.

"Directions to your place?" Scott asked.

He lived in Kensington, so I told him to take
Connecticut to University Boulevard, University
to Georgia Avenue, Georgia to our street. . . .

"We're the house with the Porta-John in the
front yard," I said.

He laughed. "You *really* go all out for Sadie
Hawkins Day, don't you?"

I laughed too. "I'm serious. We're remodeling, and the workmen are still there."

"Okay, I'll find you," he said. "If no one
answers the door, I'll try the Porta-John."

Why can't real life be more like the movies?
Why couldn't the new addition be finished, the
crew gone? Why couldn't Dad invite Scott inside
and lead him back to our new family room, where
a fire would be crackling in our big stone fireplace and Sylvia would be sitting beside it with
Annabelle in her lap?

Now I didn't want him to come in! The
dining-room furniture was squeezed into the
living room, and there was only a narrow path

leading to the stairs. The first thing Scott would see when he walked in the door was our refrigerator!

Then I thought of Molly and how she would probably give anything just to be well and going to the dance at all. The condition of her house would be the last thing on her mind.

I don't know exactly how she works it, but whenever Jacki Severn writes a feature article herself, she manages to make the front page. At least, her articles start there, along with her byline. We put out a paper every two weeks, and it's only eight pages long. Except for a controversial feature article I wrote last semester, "The City at Night," my articles have always appeared near the back. I wished that Scott would be a little more forceful.

The thing that really got to me—and some of the others, too—was that Jacki sometimes added little spot illustrations to her stories that she picked up off the Internet: a couple dancing, a girl with a book, a dog, a boat—whatever she was writing about. And if you counted up characters per line, one little piece of clip art took up three or four lines, but those never seemed to figure in *her* word count. She made the rest of us cut three or four lines when *we* went over, though.

When the paper came out this time, however,

Jacki was steaming. As we were getting ready to distribute them to the homerooms before school on Tuesday morning, she marched over to Scott and said, "Okay, where are they?"

"They?" said Scott.

"The heart motifs."

"We had to take them out, Jacki—we got a new ad and needed the space. They took up too much room, and besides, Valentine's Day is over," he said.

"My article was about relationships!" she said.

"We need every ad we can get," Scott replied.

"You didn't even tell me!" Jacki said, her voice rising. "I *am* the features editor, you know!"

And now Scott's voice had an edge to it. Microscopic, maybe, but I could tell. "You weren't here when we did the final layout, remember? The ad came in just before our deadline, and removing that spot seemed the best way to get the space."

Yay, Scott! I was thinking.

"Well, next time I don't want anyone tinkering with my articles," Jacki said, and she included all of us in her sweeping glare.

Miss Ames had come in halfway through her tirade. "The thing is, Jacki," she said, "that clip art does take up space, and we needed to cut somewhere."

"I thought they added a lot to my articles! To the paper!" Jacki protested.

Miss Ames smiled. "In a perfect world, where we could put out as big a paper as we wanted, yes. But that's just not the case."

Jacki gave an indignant sigh, grabbed up her bundle of papers to distribute, and stormed out.

"Whew!" said Don. "Has the temperature gone up a couple degrees?"

The rest of us chuckled and picked up our bundles, and Scott and I exchanged smiles as I left for the homerooms in the west corridor.

Liz seemed to have forgotten that she'd been upset with me when I told her I had a date for the dance with Scott, as though I'd been bragging or something. On the morning of the dance, as we were riding to school, she asked what I'd be wearing.

"My good jeans with a big red patch on the butt," I said. "And I sewed some patches on a peasant blouse. For a while I even thought about wearing a black bonnet with a corncob pipe in my mouth and going as Mammy Yokum."

"Now, *that* would be a hit!" Liz laughed.

When we walked inside the building, we heard laughing and shrieking up and down the halls, and we saw that someone had scattered straw here and there in the corridors. And then we saw the chickens—a dozen hens, maybe, all clucking and squawking and skittering down the tile floors.

"What is this?" we laughed, but nobody seemed to know, except that a big hand-lettered sign just inside the entrance read DOGPATCH TONIGHT.

Some of the teachers thought it was funny, but the principal didn't, and the custodian liked it least of all. We were pretty sure the dance committee had pulled the stunt, but finally the senior class president got on the mike and announced that anyone who caught and delivered a chicken to the custodian's room would get free admission to the Sadie Hawkins Day dance. Within fifteen minutes, each of the dozen hens had been cornered in a stairwell or a classroom, and the school eventually settled down.

I doubt that anyone will forget the first Sadie Hawkins Day we ever had—the morning, anyway. And when I saw Don in the hall later, he said, "I got some great pictures for the yearbook!"

5

Stupefyin' Jones

I was ready to leave the minute Scott rang the bell that evening, because I didn't want him to have to be inside our messy house one second longer than necessary. He was grinning when I opened the door.

"Got any chickens you need rounding up, ma'am?" he asked.

"Scott, were you the one who let those loose at school?" I said, laughing.

"No, but I know who did. *The Edge* never reveals its sources, though."

I realized it would be impolite not to invite him in, so I said, "Want to come in for a sec?"

He stepped in the microscopic space just inside the door. "Wow! These *are* close quarters, aren't they?"

"*Told* you!" I said, and called, "Dad? Sylvia? We're leaving."

They came downstairs—Dad in his bulky knit sweater and Sylvia in a turquoise sweatpants set. She had her camera.

"Hello, Scott," said Dad genially, shaking his hand, and Sylvia gave him a nice smile.

"Great costumes, you guys," she said. "Sounds like a fun evening."

"A new experience, anyway," said Scott. "Nice to meet you both."

I didn't know if he meant that it was me or the dance that was a new experience, but he was dressed for it, all right. He was wearing overalls over a knit polo shirt with heavy work boots on his feet.

"Ready?" he asked.

"Let me snap a picture first, and then I'll let you go," Sylvia said.

We paused in the doorway for the flash. Then I threw on an old jacket with patches sewn on the sleeves, we said our good-byes, and we walked across the wood plank sidewalk on the front lawn. I guess I could be grateful I wasn't wearing a floor-length gown, trailing in the muddy snow, but it was still humiliating. Even more so when I opened the car door and heard a girl's voice saying, ". . . but in their front *yard*?" I knew that Christy Levin had spotted the Porta-John.

I couldn't see her face very well as I slid in

the front seat. The light went off again as Scott closed my door, but I did get a glimpse of a brunette with a topknot on her head, finely arched eyebrows, and a bright red mouth.

"Hey, Alice!" said Don.

"Hi, Don. Hi, Christy," I said, and immediately wondered why Scott had picked me up last.

As Scott started the car, he said, "They're in my neighborhood, so I picked them up first."

"Anyone heard of this band? The Yokum Hokem?" asked Christy.

Don laughed. "Probably just a bunch of guys who change their name for every event."

"Did you bring your camera, or are you off duty tonight?" Scott asked him.

"Off duty, man! Sam's going to take the pictures," Don said.

Great. I was going to this dance with my crush, Scott Lynch; my ex-boyfriend, Sam Mayer, was taking pictures; and I had a date to the prom with my former boyfriend, Patrick Long. Did I even have a clue about what was really going on inside my head?

It was a fun band, whether they had an official name or not: two fiddles, a guitar, drums, an accordion, and a harmonica player who also strummed a washboard with metal picks on his fingers.

There were no live chickens this time, but the art class had painted a large backdrop behind the band—a log cabin with a crooked chimney, a couple pigs in the foreground, and a winding path leading up into the mountains.

And around the edge of the gym were all sorts of fun stuff from the comic strip: a "Kickapoo Joy Juice" stand; a bowling alley with Schmoos for pins; a cave for Lonesome Polecat and Hairless Joe; a corner named Lower Slobbovia. Different members of the Drama Club wandered about the gym, dressed as Al Capp characters: Moonbeam McSwine, General Bullmoose, Pappy Yokum, Senator Phogbound, Joe Btfsplk, and Appassionata von Climax.

Most of the girls came in Daisy Mae Scragg's off-the-shoulder tops, paired with either tight jeans or short, tight skirts. A lot of the guys tried to look like Li'l Abner, with his big shock of hair in front. But nobody really cared. Any article of clothing with a patch on it would do.

Pamela and Tim came the closest to looking like the real thing. Somewhere Tim had got overalls with only one strap across the shoulder.

"Hey, Tim! Way to go!" I said, and we all clapped when they were declared the Best Dogpatch Look-Alikes—even better than Jill and Justin, who usually win the prize for any couples' event.

And then there was the dancing. Of all the times I'd worked with Scott on the newspaper, all the times we'd leaned over a layout or stacked bundles of newspapers in each other's arms or sat together in the sub shop waiting for the printed copies from next door—none of those times were we face-to-face, our bodies only an inch apart, hand in hand.

The first time he slid one hand behind my back and took my other hand in his, my heart leaped like a startled cricket. I was almost afraid he could feel it.

When we weren't dancing, we wandered around the gym, posed for photos with "Marryin' Sam" (Sam Mayer), me with a short little bridal veil on my head, Scott with a coonskin cap. Sam was still friendly with me, and I'm glad, because it would have been awkward working together on the paper if he wasn't. As long as Sam has a girlfriend, he's fine, and he was going out with a sophomore now, who adored him.

We watched the Jumping Frog contest and the Spittin' contest, and Christy and I sat down in a booth to listen to Mammy Yokum give a two-minute lecture called "Now That You've Got Your

Man, What Are You Goin' to Do with 'im?"

Mammy Yokum was another member of the Drama Club, a short girl in a black bonnet, black fitted jacket, tight skirt, and striped stockings. She was really good. She talked with a corncob pipe dangling out one side of her mouth.

"This har's mah advice," she said. "Keep his stomach full, his hair cut, his toenails trimmed, his bed warm, and his dog fed, and ya'll won't have no trouble."

"And if he's out chasing other women?" Christy asked, to keep her going.

"Honey, he run so long and so fast afore you caught 'im, he's not about to go runnin' agin," Mammy Yokum said.

We paid her with the "Rasbuckniks" that were given out as we entered the gym. The sign said that one Rasbucknik was worth nothing, and a bunch was worth even less due to the trouble of carrying them around.

We were about to try on some "Wolf Gal" fashions when Sean Murphy, chairman of the dance committee, took the mike, and a drumroll got the kids' attention.

"Hey, y'all," he shouted. "How ya doin'?" And after a few introductory jokes he said he was about to announce an unannounced event. We quieted down, and he continued: "As you know,

Sadie Hawkins Day was established to help every gal get her man. Now, I don't know how many of you guys was roped and hog-tied into comin' or how many of you came willingly—*eagerly*, even. But it wouldn't be Sadie Hawkins Day without a bona fide, gen-u-ine, all-leather, one hundred percent natural Sadie Hawkins Day race!"

We all looked around, wondering if we were going to have to chase our dates.

"But relax, men," Sean continued. "You guys out there have already been caught. I want y'all to stand back now, clear a big open space—the whole basketball court, to be exact—'cause Earthquake McGoon here, the world's dirtiest wrassler . . ." He stepped aside as a rough-looking guy walked through the gym door behind him, holding his arms up in a victory salute. ". . . is going to be chased by the one and only, the most beautiful, most gorgeous *Stupefyin' Jones!*"

The gym door opened again, and in came a girl in a long black wig, sleekly curled, and a skimpy dress made of leaves or something. The plunging neckline exposed the top of her bulging breasts.

All the guys whistled and clapped.

I could only stare. Pamela, standing a few feet away, was staring too. Who *was* it? Somehow she looked familiar. . . .

And then Pamela gasped: "Omigod! It's *Elizabeth*!"

It was.

There are some things just too hard to believe. The breasts, for one! But there she stood, barefoot, one hand on her hip, looking seductively out over the crowd.

"Now, we all know that Stupefyin' Jones, according to Al Capp," Sean went on, "was so drop-dead gorgeous that she could literally freeze men in their tracks, just at the sight of her."

Here Earthquake McGoon glanced over at Liz and immediately stood motionless, mouth hanging open, eyes unblinking.

"So you might think," said Sean, as McGoon began to breathe again, "that she could have almost any man she wanted in Dogpatch. But sometimes there's a shortage of men, and even the most beautiful, the most voluptuous . . ."—here Liz let her fingers slide slowly down her body as Pamela and I shrieked with laughter—". . . is liable to get a little desperate." Liz's feet pawed at the ground, and she licked her lips as she leaned toward Earthquake McGoon.

"So this is it, folks. The big race! Earthquake McGoon, in a race for his life and his bachelorhood, versus the beautiful, the sexy, the fabulous Stupefyin' Jones! Let's hear it, everybody!"

We all cheered and whooped like mad, but . . . We still couldn't believe it. *Elizabeth?* Why? How? When? Who had persuaded her?

Everyone backed up a little and jockeyed for a good place to watch the race.

"Ready?" Sean said. "Take your places."

Earthquake McGoon scratched his belly and moved a couple yards in front of Liz.

"Set!" Sean called.

Both McGoon and Jones bent in the usual racer's stance.

"Go!" Sean yelled, and somebody fired a blank.

McGoon started running, Jones close behind, and it was obvious that this was a comedy act they had rehearsed. He would stumble, she'd almost catch him, he'd speed up, she'd be close behind. . . . Around the gym they went, Sean keeping up a commentator's rap: "And Jones is gaining, she's gaining, folks . . . around the bend and . . . Oops! Jones almost stumbles, but she's off again, and . . . Wait! Where's McGoon? Where the heck did he go?"

Detouring around the bleachers, McGoon was in and out of the crowd, everyone shrieking, urging them on. Once or twice Liz almost had him, but McGoon escaped her grasp. At long last, she caught him by the back of his pants, and down he went, yelping, braying, howling, pleading.

When he finally lay still, Stupefyin' Jones bent down to kiss him. Then—her face full of revulsion—she stood up again, holding her nose, and with a rejecting wave of her hand, walked away.

Everybody cheered again, whistling and clapping.

"Can you *believe* this?" I cried to Pamela. "Can you believe *her*?"

"She never said one word!" Pamela gasped.

"Isn't she the girl who went with you to do that feature story last year?" asked Scott.

"Yes!" I said. "I still can't believe this."

"A girl of many talents," said Scott.

"And she just joined the girls' track team!" I said in amazement.

"Not surprised," said Scott.

What was it like for Liz, out there in front of everybody, getting applause, everyone cheering? I wondered. For a moment I wished *I* were Liz, yet I hated to think I was jealous.

While the race had been going on, the buffet table opened behind us. Now people were moving toward the food, and I told Scott I'd join him in a minute. But first Pamela and I just had to find Liz, and we saw her, all right, with kids gathered around her, Liz all smiles.

All we could say when we grabbed her was "Liz!"

The three of us laughed, and her eyes just sparkled.

"You knew all the time you'd be here?" I asked.

"No, only a week ago," she said. Then she told us how Sean had called her and said they were looking for a girl from the track team to play Stupefyin' Jones, and someone had suggested her.

"But I just joined a month ago," she'd told him, and Sean had said never mind, he'd seen her picture. Would she do it? "My first thought was no, because I'd never heard of the character," Liz continued, "but when he said she was drop-dead gorgeous and all I had to do was run, I thought, 'I can do that!' So then we practiced, and I had a ball. It was so much fun! And it didn't matter if anyone laughed at me, because they were *supposed* to laugh."

"You were great!" Pam said.

"I was mostly afraid I'd fall, but they said that whatever happened, just make it part of the act, and it worked."

"Wow, Liz. What a part!" I told her. "You're a natural comedian! But . . ." My eyes dropped to her breasts. "How . . . ?"

She caught my arm and whispered, "Shhh. It's a push-up bra."

"Well, it . . . and *you* were fabulous," said Pamela.

Some guys were coming over to talk to Liz, so Pam went back to find Tim and I joined Scott in the buffet line. There were buffalo wings and smoked sausages, biscuits, corn, and blueberry pie. We sat on folding chairs along one side of the gym, and other kids crawled up in the bleachers. I hadn't had a chance to really talk much with Christy, so I took the chair next to hers. But she and Don were discussing a foreign film they'd seen, so I didn't have anything to add to the conversation.

Scott and I made another round of the gym, looking for things worth mentioning in a write-up. We stopped at the GSA table to look at the group's new brochure, and Scott talked with Phil and Lori about how many schools have a Gay/Straight Alliance.

Then the music started again and people began dancing. Christy and Don went back out on the floor. I went to the restroom and rinsed my mouth, put on fresh lip gloss, relined my eyes. When I went back upstairs, the music was slower, a bit more romantic. When Scott led me onto the floor, I waited for that little squeeze of the hand that meant he was enjoying himself, the tightening of his arm around my waist, an almost imperceptible tugging, pulling me toward him. . . .

It didn't happen, though. He smiled at me a lot, but it also seemed as though his eyes looked over my shoulder much of the time. He was polite, he was gallant, he was all the things a date should be. But I could tell he just wasn't all that excited by me.

A half hour before the dance was to end, he told me that Don and Christy wanted to leave, did I mind? I guess I didn't. I think I was ready for the evening to end. But it didn't.

"We're going for coffee, Alice. That okay?" Scott asked. "Starbucks is still open."

"Sure," I said. At least they had invited me. They could have taken me home first and gone out, just the three of them, and talked about what a drag I'd been, I suppose. So I put on my happy face and ordered a caramel latte with extra cream. Why did I get the feeling that somebody else was in control of the evening? That I was sort of here by default, because I'd paid for Scott's ticket?

I guess Christy's the type of girl you'd call handsome, not beautiful. An interesting face. Deep-set eyes topped by those carefully plucked eyebrows. A fine thin nose. Exceptionally white teeth. I wondered what she thought of me.

"Hope Sam got some good shots," Scott said to me over his triple mocha. "There were sure plenty of photo ops. We'll do a double-page spread on the dance."

"You write for the paper too?" Christy asked me, meaning that Scott had probably not talked about me at all on the way over. Maybe I wasn't worth mentioning. A byline wasn't exactly an attention-getter, nothing like running around the gym in a push-up bra.

Scott answered for me. "She sure does. Alice wrote that 'City at Night' piece last fall. Oops. We're supposed to keep that one anonymous."

"The article about two girls out on the town at night?" said Christy. "It was sort of . . . anti-climactic, wasn't it?"

"Well, it wasn't fiction, you know," said Scott.

"It had its moments," said Don. "Especially when that car full of guys stopped. . . ."

Christy just smiled at me indulgently. Then, turning to Scott, she said, "Any word from colleges yet?"

"Nope," he said. "I've applied to four, so we'll see what happens."

"I already know where I'm going," said Don. "Montgomery College. My dad says it doesn't really matter where you go the first two years as long as your grades are good. Get an associate degree, then transfer to a really good school, graduate from there. Save a heap of money."

"That's what my brother did, and he's getting his master's this spring," I volunteered, glad to be part of the conversation.

"Really," said Christy. "What's his major?"

"Philosophy," I told her.

"I'm impressed," said Don.

"So am I," I said, and everyone smiled.

But that was my last contribution for the evening, because the talk turned to student loans, where to get the best deals on used cars, then a film festival that all three of them had attended in Baltimore. Somehow the conversation always seemed about two steps ahead of me, just beyond my reach. Whatever I felt I had to add seemed ordinary, even juvenile, at times. So I kept quiet.

Was it just me feeling insecure? Or did one extra year of high school make that much difference? I wondered.

I'd have to describe the end of the evening as uneventful. Nobody said anything rude. I couldn't even say I was ignored. It was just that they could sort of take me or leave me, like it was okay if I was there and okay if I wasn't.

When it was time to leave at last, Scott helped me on with my jacket and kidded around a little with the girl at the counter who asked about our costumes.

"Fun evening, Alice," Scott said as he walked me up to our porch. "Thanks for the invitation."

"I'm glad you could come," I said. I didn't have to wonder if I should invite him in, because Don and Christy were waiting for him out in the car. "Good night, Scott," I said, looking up at him.

"G'night," he said, and kissed me on the forehead. The forehead! Like I was eleven years old or something. He squeezed my hand, then trotted back down the steps, across the board sidewalk to the street, and as he opened his door, I opened mine. They closed at exactly the same time.

6

Intimate Conversation

The best part of having a new adventure is telling your friends. Even a bummer can have the makings of a good story. For Elizabeth, the Sadie Hawkins Day dance was a terrific tale she could tell again and again. But for me, the dance was a sort of nonevent. There was no romance to report, no huge embarrassment to share.

At the Melody Inn the next morning, I wished I hadn't told anyone I was going to the dance. Both Marilyn, Dad's assistant manager, and David were watching for me, anticipation in their eyes.

"No," I said, giving them what I hoped was a wry smile as I slipped my bag under the counter.

"Oh?" said Marilyn.

"Neither good nor bad."

"Okay," she said, and knew enough not to ask more.

"A blah sort of evening," I told David. "Nothing spectacular either way."

"It happens," he said.

Dad and Sylvia had been curious, of course, but mostly I talked about Liz and how funny and fabulous she had been. They laughed at my description of the big race. When I told them that Scott and Don and Christy and I had gone to Starbucks later, and that Scott brought me home first, that seemed to answer whatever else Dad needed to know. But I could tell from Sylvia's eyes that being brought home first, when your date is doing the driving, is not a good thing.

"Well," she said, in a confidential whisper, "you have the prom to look forward to, don't you?"

"Yes!" I said. She understood.

Pamela invited Liz and me to her house for a sleepover that evening so we could talk about the dance. I figured we'd chill out in Pamela's bedroom, but when I got there, Mr. Jones and Meredith—the woman he's engaged to—said they were going into D.C. for dinner and a show, and Meredith had left taco fixings for us. So we sprawled out on the living-room rug instead.

"I can't wait until our remodeling is finished and I can invite you over," I told them.

"Neither can we!" said Pamela. "It's been ages since I've been inside your house. When will they be finished?"

"A couple of weeks, they're telling us. At least, that's when the plastic sheets come down and we can start moving our stuff into the new addition."

"Did you invite Scott to come in?" asked Liz.

"Are you kidding? I was ready to go the minute he came to the door," I joked, and immediately changed the subject. "Liz, when did you get to the dance? What did they do—keep you hidden until the big moment? And why didn't you *tell* us?"

She giggled. "I waited until they called, and then Dad drove me over. They told me not to tell *any*one about the race, so I didn't."

"Well, you sure had a crowd around you the last time I checked," said Pamela, grinning. "Mostly guys, too!"

Liz was positively radiant. "You know what one boy said to me? 'I never would have suspected.' I asked what he meant by that, and he looked embarrassed. He just mumbled something about how funny I was, but later—when the music started again—he came back and we danced."

"Well! Liz!" I said, smiling. "Who was he?"

"I didn't even get his name. Another guy came over, and then I danced with him."

Pamela and I beamed at her like proud mamas. The next best thing to having a great evening yourself is seeing one of your friends, who really needs it, having a good time. And then we noticed that Liz looked a bit—well, more than a bit—fuller under her crewneck T-shirt.

"Keeping a little reminder of the Sadie Hawkins Day dance?" I said, nodding toward her chest.

She laughed. "Yeah. I thought I'd try out the push-up bra, get a little more use out of it. Unless it's false advertising."

"Hey, guys will like you for more than that," I said.

"Let's hope," said Elizabeth.

Pamela turned her attention to me. "Soooo," she said, dumping another spoonful of meat in a taco shell, then heaping on the cheese. She took a crunchy bite and chewed for a minute. "How'd it go with Scott?"

I didn't want to prolong the pain. "It was just an okay evening," I said. "We went to Starbucks afterward with Don and Christy, then he brought me home. *Before* he took them home."

Pamela winced. "Ouch," she said.

"I know." I idly ran my finger over my plate, picking up the odd bits of cheese.

"No . . . sparks?" asked Liz.

"Not really. We danced. He was sweet. Attentive. Friendly. How's that? No cheek-to-cheek dancing. No hand squeezes."

"What happened when he got you home?" asked Pamela, as though if she kept at it long enough, she could extract *some*thing.

I sighed. "He kissed me on the forehead."

Pam and Liz both groaned.

"But it's a *start,* maybe," Liz said encouragingly.

"Well, if he had to start somewhere, I'd suggest farther down," said Pamela, and at least that made us laugh. If you can laugh with your girlfriends, you don't feel all that bad.

"Did he at least have a good time?" Liz asked.

"I think so. He liked all the stuff connected to Sadie Hawkins—we all did. The Schmoo bowling alley and stuff. The food was good. He liked the conversation with Don and Christy about colleges and student loans and stuff, but I was more or less a bystander. I mean, what do I know?"

"So there just wasn't any . . . guy/girl sort of feeling? On his part, I mean? Nothing sexy?" asked Pamela.

"I'd say it was more just friends," I said ruefully.

We sat quietly for a few moments.

"I saw him stop at the GSA table," said Pamela. "Maybe he's gay."

"Maybe he's *not*!" I said. "He took a girl to the Snow Ball. Maybe it's *me*. Why is it that whenever a guy doesn't pay attention to a girl, some girls assume he must be gay?"

"I didn't say there was anything wrong with it," Pamela said.

"Of course there isn't, but why can't it be that he's just not that into me? Period."

"Then why did he agree to go?" asked Liz.

"Maybe he wasn't sure how he felt about me. Maybe he was just curious. Maybe he hoped bells would ring and violins would play, and it didn't happen. Who knows?"

"But . . . what's not to like, Alice? You looked wonderful!" said Pamela.

That made me laugh in spite of myself. "So did a hundred other girls. You don't fall for every guy just because he looks good and is interested in you, do you?" My eyes narrowed. "*Do* you?"

"Is that a trick question?" Pamela asked, and we laughed.

She settled back against the cushions we'd propped against the couch. "I think I'm just plain lucky to have Tim, because it's not just looks that matter to us. We talk a lot. I've never liked a guy as much as I like Tim, you know?"

I grinned. "I know it. If you'd been dancing any closer, you'd have been joined by osmosis."

Pamela glanced at me quickly and there was something about her face, her smile. . . .

"Pamela?" I said.

She pretended to wipe her mouth, but I think she was trying to disguise her smile. "Yeah, we're close," she said.

I studied her. "How close is *close*?"

"Close," said Pamela.

Liz looked as though she were holding her breath. "*Close* close?" she asked.

"*Close* close," said Pamela. Anyone listening to our conversation would have thought we were insane.

"You . . . you . . . did *it*?" I asked, and I'm not sure why I was surprised, but I was. I mean, we had promised each other once, the three of us, that whoever had sex first—intercourse, I mean—would tell the others what it was like.

"Oh . . . my . . . God!" Liz gasped.

"Wow!" I said.

"And you didn't *tell* us?" Liz cried.

Pamela laughed. "I wasn't about to ask your permission."

"*When?*" I said. "For how long?"

"Two months ago," Pamela told us, smiling down at her hands. "And six or seven times since."

"Whew!" I said, trying hard to take it all in.

Liz was still astonished. "*Where?*"

"Here. Dad works until six, you know. Tim's house sometimes. And, yes, Liz, quit looking at me like that. We do use condoms, if that's what you were about to ask."

Liz giggled.

What to ask? Man, oh, man, this was important. This was education. This was . . . *Pamela!*

"Okay, tell all," I said. "What was it like?"

There was a sparkle in her eyes. "Well, imagine waves crashing against the shore and fireworks going off and an avalanche," she said.

"*That's* what it's like?" asked Liz.

"No," said Pamela, and we giggled some more. "It isn't like any of that. But it's exciting and it feels good and it's a little frustrating and you don't want it to stop. And just thinking about doing it makes you want to do it again."

I was trying to put those pieces together and come out with an "experience," but I was having a hard time of it. I began to wonder if we should be asking all these personal questions. I wanted details, but it also seemed very private. I was sure it was private when Pamela said, "I figure it gets better with time. We're still exploring . . ."—she broke into a smile again—". . . and that's the fun part."

We knew then that the question period was over, but Liz had one more: "Just tell me this: The first time, does it hurt?"

"Yeah. Enough that I made him stop. I was bleeding a little. We tried again later. Once you heal, though, after a couple of days, you're fine. It's sort of like a little cut down there."

Liz pushed back against the pillows and thrust both hands between her legs. "That's it. I'm going to be a nun," she said.

"No, you're not. You'll love it. Choose a gentle guy, though. Don't let it be someone like Brian."

We both looked at her. "Brian Brewster? Did he ever . . . ?"

"No, but he wanted to. I can't imagine Brian being gentle with anyone."

We thought about that a moment.

"You know, I thought he might change after the accident," said Liz. "I really thought that he'd think about that little girl and what the accident might mean for the rest of her life, but he's just been a cranky bore. All he does is complain because he can't drive for a year."

"It's like he goes around with a big 'Me' sign

on his shirt," I added. "If Brian was religious, he'd worship himself. It's as though that little girl is an obstacle to his career. 'Man, I've got things to do!' he says. 'This is my junior year. It's not like I purposely tried to hurt someone.'"

We groaned.

"You know what I heard?" said Pamela. "Keeno told me that Brian's dad promised him a new car if he'd just wait out the year without getting in any more trouble. A *new car!*"

Keeno, a friend of Brian's from another school, probably knows him better than anyone else. Sometimes he goes to the movies with us. But I think maybe he's getting a little sick of Brian too.

"Oh, man!" I said.

"Anyone ever meet his dad? Maybe he's just as self-centered as Brian," said Liz. "I've heard that if you want to know what your future husband will be like in twenty years, take a look at his dad. I suppose that goes for a girl, too—she'll be like her mother. Which means that any guy who is serious about me should study my mom. Now *there's* a sobering thought."

Pamela rolled her eyes. "God forbid! Or *mine!*"

I was the only one who didn't say anything. I couldn't even understand the feeling. I would give anything in this world to be like my mother. To *see* my mother. To know what she had really been like.

By the time I went to school on Monday, I began to feel that my crush on Scott was fading. There's something about knowing for sure that you aren't special to somebody that both breaks your heart and frees you. Or maybe I'm just the kind of girl who doesn't go after the unattainable. I've never been nuts over a celebrity—guys I know I'll never have or perhaps wouldn't even like if I got to know them.

If Scott had loved me madly once and now he didn't, that would be one thing. If I had rejected him and now I wanted him back, that would be different too. But when I saw him at his locker Monday and stopped by to say hello, and he smiled that same friendly, platonic smile as before, I didn't feel my pulse speed up the way I used to. Just a little ache.

The romance wasn't over, because it had never really begun. What I mean is, *I* was over it. I no longer imagined that his smile meant something personal. And when we had our next staff meeting for *The Edge* on Wednesday, I didn't get the familiar *ting* when we worked side by side and our arms touched. I *had* been crushing on him, but there was also a wisp of a thought that I'd wanted to go out with him at least once to compare him to Patrick—to see what kind of guy I preferred. No, I was definitely over him. I think. . . .

Two months ago, I thought I had a handle on who I was. Now I wasn't so sure.

Lester called that night and I was trying to explain it to him. He'd wanted to ask Dad about something, but Dad wasn't home, and he got me instead.

"I used to think I knew the real Alice," I told him. "'Almost Alice' is more like it. I'm not absolutely positive I'm over Scott; I'm not completely sure that Patrick and I are right for each other, and if we are, how serious we should get; I wish I could do something wild and funny like Liz did at the dance, but I don't know if it's really me. . . ."

"Why do you have to have the answers to any of this right now?" Les asked me.

"I just want to be sure of *some*thing, Lester! If I can't be sure about a guy, can't I at least be sure of myself?"

"But *why*?" he asked. "Why do you have to have your future all wrapped up like a Christmas present, ready for you to open when you're twenty-five or something? Why can't you just relax and let things happen?"

"I don't know," I answered. "I just can't."

7

Pushing Pamela

When you can't figure yourself out, you concentrate on friends, and that's why I now focused on Pamela. Liz and Gwen and I were determined that she try out for a part in the spring musical, *Guys and Dolls*, to be performed the last two weekends in April. A sign-up sheet for auditions was posted outside the choir room, and anyone could ask to borrow a copy of the songs and to try out between March 10 and 12. The cast would be posted on Friday, March 14.

It's weird about Pamela. In elementary school she was a real show-off and loved being the center of attention. She always said she wanted to be an actress or a model, and she got the lead in our sixth-grade play. In high school she joined the Drama Club in her freshman year, then dropped out the second semester. She said she couldn't possibly compete with all those talented people. I

finally persuaded her to sign up again last year—
just for stage crew along with me—and she did.
But even though she's been taking voice lessons,
she still doesn't feel she's "good enough" to try for
anything more.

Liz and Gwen and I decided to change all
that.

First, I called Tim. "We need your help," I
said. "We want to persuade Pamela to try out for
Guys and Dolls, but she really needs a push. Do
you think you could talk her into it?"

"I suggested it myself," he said. "She sings
when she's around me. She sings around you
guys. She sings along with the car radio. But
when I try to get her to—you know—really perform, she clams up. I'll see what I can do."

Next, Liz invited Pamela and Tim and Gwen
and me to her house on Friday night just to hang
out—watch a DVD or something, she said. Gwen
had signed out a book of songs from *Guys and
Dolls* and brought it along with her.

"One guy and four girls?" Pamela had asked
when Liz told her who was coming.

"I'll let my little brother hang with us," Liz
joked.

It was Tim who brought the video of *Guys
and Dolls,* starring Frank Sinatra, Jean Simmons,

Vivian Blaine, and Marlon Brando, who, would you believe, sang "Luck Be a Lady."

"Hey! What *is* this?" Pamela asked suspiciously as the credits rolled on the screen and we passed the popcorn around.

"Stage crew's supposed to watch it, remember?" I said. "Get some idea of what we'll be dealing with." We watched the singers and dancers converge on Times Square. The story, of course, is about a gambler who bets another that he can't get a date with the pretty Salvation Army–type sergeant, Sarah Brown.

"We just want to get you interested, Pamela, that's all," Liz said. "You can sing! You can dance! You can act! You're a natural!"

Pamela only laughed and answered in a Brooklyn accent, just like the character Adelaide: "Aw, youse guiys, quit ya kiddin'." We laughed.

To tell the truth, we were only thinking about Pamela being in the chorus line when the movie began.

"Hey, Pamela, you can do that!" Liz would say when a dancer kicked up one leg.

"And don't tell us you can't sing like that," Gwen said when Sister Sarah began "Follow the Fold."

We shrieked and cried, "Oh, Pamela, that's

you!" when the chorus girls, dressed like sexy cats, sang "Pet Me, Poppa," even though we didn't know how much of the movie version or even the Broadway performance would make it into the script of a high school musical.

But we got quieter as the movie went on, and I think we all began to realize that not only was Pamela right for the chorus, but she would be great for the part of Adelaide, Nathan Detroit's girlfriend, who's been trying for fourteen years to get him to marry her.

Pamela has short blond hair like Adelaide's; she's cute, like Adelaide; and—like Adelaide—Pamela can sing up a storm. If she didn't chicken out, that is.

When Gwen finally put it into words—"Pamela, Adelaide is *you*!"—we all began talking at once. Every time Pamela raised an objection, we threw popcorn at her. Liz's three-year-old brother heard the commotion and ran in to join the fun.

We watched the movie through to the end, of course, but whenever the ditzy Adelaide sang another song, especially "Adelaide's Lament," we knew just how right the whole musical was for our beloved, ditzy, risk-taking, act-without-thinking Pamela.

"All right already! I'll sign up for the chorus!" she said finally, and at least that was a start.

When Monday came, we all escorted her down to the sign-up sheet to witness her signature for the chorus. It wasn't till the next day that Pamela discovered Tim had signed her up to audition for Adelaide, too.

Patrick didn't think we ought to have done that.

We've talked once since he got home from that thing in Baltimore. He asked how the dance went and—can you believe this?—whether Scott was a good dancer, and I said it went fine and I had no complaints about Scott's dancing. That's all he wanted to know, which was disappointing. I was still smarting from that.

"I didn't sign Pamela up for the Adelaide audition," I said. "It was Tim."

"But you're all pushing her. I think that when she's ready to try out for a part, she'll do it," Patrick said.

Sometimes he really gets on my nerves. I'd been lying on my back on the bed, but now I propped myself up on one elbow, holding the phone to my ear. "Patrick, you've probably never had to be pushed to do anything in your life except eat broccoli," I said. "You're so motivated, you could move a mountain, but not everyone is like you. Right now Pamela needs all the support she can get."

"Have you ever thought that maybe the more you reassure her, the more she might feel she needs it?" Patrick said. "If you just said, 'Pamela, you know you can do it, and it's up to you whether or not you audition,' it might make her feel more confident?"

I wasn't sure of anything except that I wanted Patrick to be a little bit jealous that I went to the dance with Scott, and if he couldn't be jealous, couldn't he at least be curious? Didn't he even wonder if Scott held me close when we danced? Kissed me? I should be the topic of conversation here, not Pamela.

"Maybe you're right," I said flatly. What did I mean to him, anyway? Maybe he just asked me to the prom because he was afraid if he put it off, he'd forget. Maybe he just wanted to make sure he had a date. Old reliable Alice.

"Anyway," Patrick went on, "the orchestra got the music for *Guys and Dolls* last week. I'll be doing percussion."

I forgot momentarily that Patrick plays the drums for both the band and the orchestra—Patrick, the master of all trades: orchestra, band, track, Chess Club, debate team. . . . Why the heck didn't he run for class president while he was at it?

"Good for you," I said.

There were a few seconds of silence, and then he asked, "Alice? Something wrong?"

"Yes," I said. "Life is so easy for you, Patrick. You succeed in everything you do while—"

"Whoa! Whoa!" he said. "Where did you get that idea?"

"But isn't it true?"

"Not by a long shot. You don't know the half of it."

I felt a little foolish then. "When will I know the other half?"

"Oh, when the time's right," said Patrick.

I didn't ask when that might be, because with Patrick, there's never enough time. But he made it sound as though he might *make* time for me somewhere down the line. I guess I'd wait.

He did have a point about Pamela. The way we kept pushing and persuading her must have made her feel as though she couldn't do it on her own. So when she called me that Tuesday night and said she was furious at Tim for putting her name on the list for Adelaide and she wasn't going to audition tomorrow, I said, "You're right, Pamela. He shouldn't have done that. And I apologize for all of us for trying to make you do something you don't want. I think you know you can sing and dance better than most of us, and we know it, but it's entirely up to you."

We didn't see her before school on Wednesday. Gwen said she checked the sign-up list, and Pamela hadn't crossed out her name for either the chorus or for Adelaide, but we didn't know if she was going to audition or not. No one else could attend the auditions—only the names on the sign-up sheet. Mr. Gage (the choir director), Mr. Ellis (the drama coach), and Miss Ortega (the dance teacher), along with a piano player, would be the only other people in the room during tryouts. They said they didn't want any cheering sections watching from the wings.

I got all this from Charlene Verona, the girl who drove everyone nuts back in ninth grade when she got the part of Tzeitel in *Fiddler on the Roof*. I hoped she wasn't trying out for the part of Adelaide and was glad when she said she auditioned to play the role of Sarah Brown.

Pamela didn't call me Wednesday night, and we didn't call her. Gwen and Liz and I made a vow we wouldn't even bring up the topic at lunch the next day. It was a struggle, though. It was Charlene, of course, who spilled the beans. She breezed by our table as we were finishing our sandwiches and said breathlessly, "We both got callbacks, Pamela! Wouldn't it be great if I played Sister Sarah and you played Adelaide?"

We looked at Pamela and began to grin.

"Way to go, girl!" said Gwen.

Gwen and I went to visit Molly after school on Thursday. She was up in her room, working at the computer, baseball cap tipped at an angle on her head.

"Hey!" Gwen said. "How you doing?"

"Busy!" Molly answered, giving us a smile.

We threw our jackets on the bed. "Homework?" I asked.

"Stage crew," said Molly. "Mr. Ellis put me in charge of props." We stared. "He called last week and asked if I wanted to be part of stage crew again this year, and I said yes. So he e-mailed me a list of all the props, and I'm seeing how many I can find for him."

"Great!" I said, sending Mr. Ellis a hug by mental telepathy. "What have you got so far?"

Molly read off some things from her screen. "The print shop's working with the auto shop to make a Times Square street sign; an art class is doing the lettering for the Save-a-Soul Mission; the band's supplying a bass drum; a church is supplying the hymnbooks; a thrift shop is loaning us some fifties dresses; and a restaurant says we can borrow two fake palm trees for the scene in Havana."

Gwen and I hooted with laughter. "Oh, Molly, you're amazing!" Gwen said.

She grinned. "That's what my doctor said."

"Really?"

"So far so good," said Molly.

"Wonderful!" we told her.

"So who's trying out?" she wanted to know. "Pamela would be so good with that music."

"Actually, she tried out for the part of Adelaide, but the cast hasn't been posted yet," I said.

"Adelaide?" shrieked Molly. "The ditzy girlfriend? The one who sings 'Take Back Your Mink'? She'd be great!"

"Yeah, but there are lots of girls trying out, and they always cast seniors when possible," I said. "But drink the rest of your milk shake and I'll show you the photos we're using in the newspaper of the Sadie Hawkins Day dance."

Molly made a face, picked up her half-full glass, and dutifully drank the rest of her shake. Then we sat together on the cushioned window seat in her bedroom and I showed her the first photo.

"Omigod!" She gasped. "Is that . . . is that Liz?"

"Stupefyin' Jones in the flesh," I said.

Gwen hadn't seen the photos yet either— they'd be coming out in the next issue of *The*

Edge—so we had some laughs. I wondered after a while whether this was helping or hurting . . . if I wasn't just reminding Molly of all the things she was missing. But she genuinely looked as though she were having a good time. And when we put the last photo back in the envelope, she said, "I plan on coming to one of the performances of *Guys and Dolls* and going onstage for a curtain call with the rest of the crew."

"Yay, Molly!" I said.

We were waiting for the official cast to be posted on Friday, the last day before spring vacation. Callbacks had been the day before, and those who were on the final list today were to pick up their scripts and music to study over the break. After we came back, there would be four weeks of rehearsals, with performances the next two weekends.

A little crowd had gathered just before homeroom, but the list wasn't up yet. I went by after first period, and it still wasn't there. Tim was checking too.

"Fingers crossed," he said.

Just before lunch, we heard that the list was up. Pamela wouldn't come. Gwen and Liz and I rushed down to the choir room and strained to see over the heads of the others. The hall was already filled now with squeals and cheers as well as murmurs of disappointment. All the big parts had gone to seniors, and a girl named Kelsey Reeves would play Adelaide. But Pamela was listed as her understudy, and she made the chorus, too.

"Do we cheer or console each other?" I asked Gwen.

"Cheer," said Gwen. "This might be just what she needed. It will give her confidence without scaring her to death."

What I was thinking, though, was that this had been Pamela's chance to shine. The school alternates each year between plays and musicals. During our freshman year, the musical was *Fiddler on the Roof*. During sophomore year, the play was *Father of the Bride*. Now it was time for a musical again, and in our senior year, it would be a play.

But I think Gwen was right about Pamela. We cheered when we saw her, and I think she was both happy and relieved. The casting group had recognized her talent without making her the center of attention.

"I've got to learn the whole thing, just like Kelsey Reeves," she said excitedly. "Same costumes and everything, except I'm in the chorus too, so I have to learn all their songs! And dance! I have to do some of the dances!"

"Say good-bye to Tim for the duration," I joked. But I was ashamed that I'd managed to stick a little needle in the celebration.

The fact was, none of us would have a lot of time over spring break. Dad asked me to work at the Melody Inn—the store was having a spring clearance sale; Pamela was memorizing Adelaide's lines and learning the songs; Liz was putting in applications for a summer job; and Gwen was working five afternoons instead of two at the health clinic.

Some kids were going on trips with their families. Karen and her mom, for instance, were going to New York, and Justin's folks were virtually kidnapping him for a trip to the Bahamas because, as Jill said, they were doing everything possible to separate her from Justin. Charlene Verona said she didn't have time to be in the musical after all (now that she didn't get a lead part) because she was getting ready for a ballet recital, and Patrick was working again part-time for the landscaper he'd worked for last summer. That left Mark Stedmeister, who was repairing an old car he was buying from his dad. I didn't know what Brian Brewster was doing, and I didn't care.

I'd promised myself I'd start looking at prom dresses over spring break, but to be honest, I dreaded it. Neither Liz nor Pam nor Gwen had been invited to this prom yet, so if we went shopping together, it would be all for me.

I'm just one of those girls who doesn't especially like to shop. I want to be gorgeous and have nice clothes; I just don't like to go looking for them and trying stuff on.

When I went to work on Saturday, I asked Marilyn what I should do. Dad's assistant manager was looking more beautiful by the day. I figured marriage had something to do with it.

"Where should I start looking?" I asked.

"Depends," said Marilyn. "What did you have in mind? Long or short? Full or slinky?"

"Long," I said. "I want to feel like I'm at a prom, not a cocktail party. I love the halter-top dress I wore to the Snow Ball, but I don't want to wear that with Patrick. But then, I don't want to spend a fortune, either."

"Maybe . . . a creamy aqua? Say . . . a form-fitting dress, simple top, spaghetti straps, three overlapping layers at the bottom, each with a two-inch satin border?"

I didn't know how anyone could mentally design a dress so fast, and I tried to visualize it. Marilyn even drew it on the back of a cash register receipt—the first layer of the skirt ending below the knee, the second layer ending mid-calf, and the third just below the ankle.

"Sold," I said. "Who sells it and how much?"

She laughed. "A friend loaned it to me, and you and I are about the same size. You can wear it if you'll dry-clean it after."

My eyes opened wide. "Marilyn! Really? I didn't think you ever dressed up!"

"I didn't think I did either, but my girlfriend of mine—a *wealthy* girlfriend—invited us to a charity ball. She told me if I'd come, she'd even loan me a dress, and the ball was last week. She's in no hurry to have the dress back. I'll ask her if you can borrow it for one night, but I'm sure it's okay."

"You're like a fairy godmother!" I squealed, hugging her.

"Hey. Try it on first. *Then* you can thank me," she said.

I told Sylvia about it when I got home, and she said we could go to Marilyn's some evening and see how it fit.

"Do you think I'm weird that I don't like to shop?" I asked her.

"No," said Sylvia. "I think your dad and I are lucky, that's what!"

• • •

We had brunch at a restaurant on Sunday and invited Les along. He happily reported that he was nearing the finish line on his thesis and would probably graduate in May. Dad was overjoyed, and we all raised our glasses to toast Lester's MA in philosophy.

I had to rib him a little, though: "That's great, Les, but can you say 'self-sup-port-ing'?"

He grinned. "Don't rush me. First things first. George Palamas is getting married in the fall, so we'll be looking for another guy to share the apartment. Meanwhile, we'd like to take off for a week if we can find someone to look after Mr. Watts."

The three men have had an agreement with old Mr. Watts, who owns the house—that they can live upstairs rent-free if they'll do odd jobs around the place and that one of them will always be there in the evenings in case Mr. Watts has an emergency. He has a nursing aide during the day.

"So where would you like to go?" asked Sylvia.

"We're looking into flying to Moab and taking a mountain bike tour," said Les.

"Moab?" I said. "Where's that? Arabia?"

Les leaned over the table. "Can you say 'U-tah,' Al?"

Frankly, my knowledge of geography really sucks. I knew there were mountains in Wyoming and Colorado, but Utah was a blank.

"I think I've failed you there," Dad said apologetically. "We didn't do much traveling as a family, did we?"

"*Much?*" said Lester. And then, realizing, I suppose, that Dad felt guilty enough, he said, "We drove from Illinois to Maryland when we moved, didn't we?"

"And we've been to Tennessee," I said, remembering the trip we made last fall just before Grandpa McKinley died. "I've been to New York and to the ocean a couple of times."

"I hope that both of you will see a lot more of the world than I have," said Dad.

Sylvia laid one hand on his arm. "We've been to England, remember."

He winked. "I was so fascinated by you that I don't even remember the rest."

"You old romantic!" she said. "Someday we're going to Paris."

That afternoon when we got home, I went to my computer and e-mailed Pamela, Liz, and Gwen:

The summer we graduate from college, i want the 4 of us 2 drive 2 california and back. Deal?

Deal, Liz e-mailed back.

Deal, agreed Pamela.

Unless I'm accepted at medical school, wrote Gwen.

8

Murder in the Mansion

Wonder of wonders, Patrick called me Monday night.

"Hi. What's happening?" he asked.

"Well, it's St. Patrick's Day, so I made some lime Jell-O. I mean, we really live it up around here," I told him. "So how are *you* celebrating? It's not everyone who has a holiday named after him."

"I'll be loading fertilizer all week," he said, "but I'd like to do at least one fun thing before spring break is over. How about going to a mystery dinner on Thursday?"

"You mean I won't know what I'm eating until I've swallowed?"

He laughed. "No, it's part of the entertainment. The waiters are part-time actors, and there's a mystery to be solved somewhere during the evening. Customers get to help solve it."

Only Patrick could think of a kitschy idea like that and not be embarrassed about it. But it sounded like fun. "Sure!" I said.

When I went to work the next day, I told Marilyn I was going out with Patrick on Thursday.

"Aha! So it's *not* just the prom! I *knew* you'd get back together!" she said.

I thought about that. "Patrick's a complex person," I said.

"Aren't we all?" said Marilyn.

Dad told us that if we'd be willing to work a couple hours overtime that night, he'd treat us to lunch at the new restaurant next door. David went with me to place the order, and we brought back Cobb salads, with cheesecake for dessert.

"Have you heard from your girlfriend lately?" I asked him back in the break room. "Or shouldn't I ask?"

"No harm in asking," said David. "I may go up there for Easter. Father Bennett asked me to be a reader at mass."

"And . . . Connie?"

"Well, I'd see her too, of course." He smiled. "She sent me a valentine last month."

"David, when you guys go out, what do you do for fun? What is there to do in New Hampshire?"

"What is there to *do*?" he exclaimed, putting

down his fork in mock horror. "You never heard of the White Mountains? Never heard of the Atlantic Ocean?"

"*Ocean?* New Hampshire's squeezed between Vermont and Maine! How can there be ocean?" I asked.

"Look at a map, Alice. We've got thirteen miles of beaches at the southern tip."

I was embarrassed. "I'm a geographic imbecile, David. I didn't know it had ocean; I didn't know it had mountains! I didn't even know there were mountains in Utah!"

"You're kidding!" said David. "Utah's one of my favorite states. You haven't seen the U.S. till you've been to Canyonlands, Arches National Park. . . . Utah's gorgeous!"

"So, back in New Hampshire, you and Connie . . . ?"

"We hike. Swim. Canoe. Camp out sometimes."

"Uh . . . separate tents?" I was pushing it, I knew.

He grinned. "Separate sleeping bags. We like old movies, classical music, Brahms. . . . We both love the church. Love poetry. Crossword puzzles. Sailing. . . ."

I studied his face. "If you give her up, won't you be lonely?"

He smiled again. "Some of the time, probably. No, absolutely, I'll miss her. But it's not as though I won't have anything to do. I'll have the whole parish. And I'll be with other priests who love the church."

I sighed and took another bite of dessert. "I guess I've never loved anyone that much. Well, my dad maybe. . . . But I can't even imagine loving a *church* so much that I'd give up all that."

"What about loving God?"

"If I ever get to that place, I'd want human love too, David."

"Many people make that choice, and it's a fine choice. But I don't just want to love, I want to be close to God . . . in a totally committed way."

I thought of David's girlfriend back in New Hampshire, waiting for his decision. Of David and Connie lying out under the stars. Canoeing, sailing, reading poetry . . . And David, okay with being alone.

"You know what I think?" I said at last. "I think you've already made up your mind, and somehow I think Connie knows it."

He was nodding his head before I'd even finished. "I think so too."

But I still couldn't understand it. Would I ever feel that absolutely committed to anything? Anyone? "I just wonder how long it takes a per-

MURDER IN THE MANSION • 109

son to really, *really* know herself," I said.

"Forever," said David. "You'll discover new things about yourself as long as you live."

"Well, that's discouraging. Every time I think I've got a handle on who I really am and what I really feel, something happens and I'm back to square one," I told him.

"That's called 'life,' Alice. You have to live with"—his fork flashed, and he swiped my last bite of cheesecake—"risk," he said.

On Wednesday evening Sylvia and I drove over to Marilyn and Jack's. Marilyn's husband is a folk guitarist, and he was putting on a children's program somewhere, so we had their little two-bedroom house in Rockville to ourselves.

Marilyn was one of Lester's first serious girlfriends, and I'd always hoped he'd marry her, but that wasn't meant to be. The original "nature girl," Marilyn usually wore cotton and sandals, and I couldn't imagine her in a long crepe dress, but there it was, all laid out on the bed.

"It's beautiful," said Sylvia. "Whoever this friend was, she had taste."

"I figure maybe I'll borrow it again for my twenty-fifth wedding anniversary or something," said Marilyn.

I'd worn my strapless bra, so I took off my

shirt and jeans, and Sylvia lowered the dress over my head and let it fall gently around my hips. The dress skimmed my legs as it fell. She zipped me up, and I turned toward the mirror.

"It's . . . gorgeous!" I breathed.

I could tell by Marilyn's and Sylvia's smiles that they thought so too.

"The straps need shortening just a bit, but I can do that without hurting the dress or making it permanent," Sylvia said. "We'll lower them again before we return it. What do you think, Marilyn?"

"I think my friend must have known somehow that I'd be generous with this dress, because she told me to keep it as long as I like," said Marilyn. "And I can't think of anyone I'd rather share it with."

I didn't dress up for the Murder Mystery Dinner Theater on Thursday, but I looked good. I was wearing the same tight jeans I'd worn to the Sadie Hawkins Day dance, minus the patches, and a cream-colored shirt.

When Patrick came to pick me up, I was still getting dressed. From down below, I heard Dad answer the door. "Well, Patrick! Good to see you! Come in, come in!" he said.

"Hi, Mr. McKinley." Patrick's voice.

A shiver of excitement went through me. How long had it been since Patrick was in our house? I wondered. Was the last time he had stepped on our porch the night we broke up? The night we walked around the neighborhood and, when I realized we were only going to make it one block, I knew it was over?

I heard Sylvia's footsteps then, and she said, "My gosh, let me get a good look at you! Patrick, you *can't* have grown a foot since you were in my class! And don't you hate it when adults talk this way?"

Patrick laughed. "Actually, I sort of like it. Not bad, looking *down* on everybody for a change."

Dad chuckled.

"Hey, *this* place has changed too," Patrick said. "New addition, huh?"

"And it's almost done," said Sylvia. "Tomorrow the men will be here to take down these horrid plastic walls, and we can move all this stuff back where it belongs."

"Sweet!" said Patrick. And here's the reason my dad likes him so much: The next thing Patrick said was, "I'm working tomorrow, but I could stop by afterward if you need any help."

"We just might," said Dad, "or we may be all moved in by then. I'm taking the day off.

Saturday, too. Stop by anyway and see what we've done to the place."

I came down then and found both Dad and Sylvia beaming. Did they really think that Patrick and I were back together again, as a couple? Didn't they know—*surely* they knew—how complicated relationships are and how little time Patrick had for me? The fact that in a few months he'd be going to the University of Chicago, a thousand miles away?

Patrick was wearing a dark red shirt, a black sweater thrown over one shoulder. I must say, we made a great-looking couple. We walked out to the car, Patrick with his hand lightly touching my waist as if to guide me along the boards that served as our sidewalk.

"Well, I guess *this* has been fun," he joked, nodding toward the Porta-John.

"Everybody makes cracks about that," I told him. "No, we didn't have to use it, thank God."

The night was gorgeous—clear sky with a three-quarters moon. Even above the lights of Silver Spring, we could see stars.

Patrick was driving his mom's car—a silver Olds. He opened the door for me and waited till I'd found the seat belt, then came around to the other side.

"Are you taking a car to Chicago?" I asked.

"Naw. I won't have a car there. I'll take Metra or grab a bus to the El if I want to go downtown. And I'll have my bike around the university."

"You're officially accepted, then?"

"Yep. Start the summer quarter. I don't even have to wait till fall," Patrick said.

That meant we wouldn't be together over the summer! But I might have known. Whenever Patrick saw a chance to get ahead, he took it. I was determined, though, that nothing would spoil the evening.

"Then tonight we're going to celebrate your going to the University of Chicago?" I asked cheerfully.

He smiled as he started the engine. "We'll celebrate whatever you want," he said.

The Blakely Mansion was a huge old brick house on the border between Silver Spring and Takoma Park. It had balconies and turrets and high narrow windows with black shutters, some of them closed.

Patrick and I walked up the steps and were greeted by a man who looked like something out of a Victorian melodrama—dark slick-backed hair, mustache, heavily painted eyebrows. He checked our reservation.

"Please follow," he said, barely smiling, and

pointed to a smaller man with a stubby beard and an eye patch. We were led to a table covered by a purple cloth, a purple candle in the center. Heavy black drapes obscured the walls and windows, and at times they rustled as though there were open doorways behind them.

Stuffed crows looked down on us from a high ledge, their steely yellow eyes seeming to catch every movement, and a thin woman in a black dress somberly plucked a harp in one corner, her black lip gloss matching her nails.

"Creepy!" I said to Patrick. "Have you been here before?"

"No, but I've heard about it. Something a little different," he said. Same thing Scott had said about going to the dance with me.

It wasn't the sort of restaurant where you gaze into each other's eyes by candlelight exactly. In elaborate script above a doorway were the words *Expect the Unexpected*. Patrick smiled at me from across the table. "Soooo?"

I smiled back. "So? Are we going to give each other an account of what we've been doing for the past week or past month or past year?"

"All of those, if you want," said Patrick.

"Well, let's see. I've grown another half inch, gained a couple pounds. I'm letting my hair grow longer, I *may* get my braces off this spring, I'm taking an accelerated course in English, and I'm running three times a week before school."

Patrick grinned. "And you're looking great," he said.

"Thank you," I told him.

A man with a Van Gogh beard and a bandaged ear brought us our menus and a black olive appetizer. We laughed at the menu. The steak was "hoary beef," the salad "plucked shoots," the dessert "black raspberries with clotted cream. . . ."

I studied Patrick as he studied the menu. His hair wasn't as fiery red as it had been back in grade school, but he had the complexion of a redhead, and his eyebrows were orange as well.

The biggest change I saw in him, though, was that he didn't talk about himself the whole time. It wasn't that he had been conceited before. It was just—well, there was always so much to tell! He was involved in so many things. But this time he was interested in Les getting his master's degree; he asked what colleges I was planning to apply to and what it was like having my seventh-grade English teacher for a mom. He even asked about Aunt Sally. I was surprised he remembered her. I started to fill him in on my relatives in Chicago when the harpist stopped playing and a man wearing a long black cape took the microphone.

In a low raspy voice he said that his name was Edgar (yes, as in Edgar Allan Poe), he welcomed us to his house, to his banquet, and asked us to please make ourselves at home. He must, however, ask us to confine ourselves to the dining room, the library, and the restrooms, for there were portions of the house, unfortunately, that were unsafe.

"I regret to inform you," he said, "that my brother, Allan"—everyone laughed—"of a somewhat deranged mentality, has escaped his quarters in the upper story and may possibly be roaming the halls. He is quite harmless unless cornered, but let me assure you that his keepers are searching for him even now. I don't wish to disturb your meal in any way, so please, please continue. . . ." And with a flourish of his cape, he disappeared behind a curtain to the applause and laughter of the guests.

As we ate our dinner, I finished telling Patrick all the news about my family—Uncle Milt's heart attack and recovery, my cousin Carol moving in with her boyfriend, and how Aunt Sally found out. Every so often we would hear muffled shouts or exclamations, and there would be movement behind one of the curtains. Once a figure darted through the dining room, chased by the cook, and somebody said, "Allan's on the loose again."

For dessert we shared a slice of devil's food cake, slathered with whipped cream. We each started at one side of the dish and smiled when our forks touched in the middle.

"The mystery starts after dinner, I think," Patrick said.

"Then I'm going to the restroom first," I told him, and picking up my purse, I asked a waiter directions to the ladies' room, then followed as he ushered me to a long hallway, with only dim lighting overhead.

I groped my way along, pausing at each closed door, looking for a LADIES sign, and finally saw it down near the end. Inside, I wished that Patrick could have seen it. There was an old bathtub on one side shaped like a coffin, and both of the sinks were empty skulls. When I sat down on the toilet seat, a groan came from beneath me, and I jumped to discover an electronic monitor that had triggered the moan of a man being crushed. I laughed out loud.

When I came out of the stall, one of the black-clad waitresses was reapplying her lip gloss. Her face was chalky white, and her eyes were heavily outlined in mascara.

"Hi," I said as I approached one of the sinks.

"*Au revoir,*" she murmured, and slunk out the door.

I put on fresh lip gloss, gave my hair a few swipes, then opened the door and started back down the hallway toward the dining room.

Suddenly a hand clamped tightly over my mouth, my arms were pinned to my sides, and before I could think, I was lifted off my feet and carried up a flight of stairs.

"Shhh," a male voice whispered. "Relax. You're part of the show. One more flight, please." And two men hustled me on up to the third floor.

All I could think about was how glad I was they had kidnapped me *after* I'd peed.

We entered a large room, a parlor of some kind, only slightly more lit than the hallway and stairs. I couldn't make out the men's faces exactly, but the guys were dressed like two of the waiters. They walked me over to a large painting on the opposite wall. One of the men pushed against it, and the painting swung open. The men hurried me through into another hallway and, from there, into another old-fashioned bathroom, with one dim light above a cracked mirror.

"Sorry about this," one of the men said, smiling apologetically, "but you worked so perfectly into the plot that we just had to make use of you. Georgene, our scullery maid, was waiting in the bathroom to see who showed up first, and we were so happy it wasn't a three-hundred-pound woman."

"What am I supposed to do?" I asked, my heart still pounding.

"Nothing at all. When it's time for you to reappear, we'll come get you," said the second waiter.

"But please don't come out before then," the first man said. "It would ruin everything."

"Can you at least tell me the plot?" I asked.

"It changes each night," he said. "But they'll start searching for you in about twenty minutes."

"The customers, you mean?" I asked.

"Yeah, but unless someone leans against that painting, they won't find you here," he said. "Try not to make any noise." He grinned again. "If you use the john, don't flush." And putting their fingers to their lips, they slipped back out again, closing the door behind them.

I looked around. The toilet was so old-fashioned, its tank was high on the wall. The claw-footed bathtub had a ring of rust around the drain, and there were little pieces of chipped plaster in the sink. I had my purse with me, but no cell phone.

And suddenly I thought of Patrick. They said I needed to be here for twenty minutes! What were they telling Patrick? Were they telling him anything at all? What if he thought I'd called a cab and gone home?

My mind raced with possibilities. What if he called my dad? What if he called the police?

Oh, sit down and enjoy it, I told myself. Except that there were only two places to sit—the edge of the tub or the toilet seat. I chose the seat. Ten minutes went by. Fifteen.

"Alice!"

It was a faraway voice. My eyes opened wide. It seemed to be coming from outdoors, but I had to crank open the window and stand on tiptoe to see the ground.

There, walking back and forth in the parking area, was Patrick, looking all around him. "Alice?" he called again. They *hadn't* told him! A few other people were milling about the veranda.

I looked around the bathroom. There were no towels to wave, no shower curtain to use as a flag. Nothing but a half roll of toilet paper sitting on the floor.

I picked it up, went back to the window again, unfurled it six or eight feet, and let it dangle. Back and forth, back and forth I moved it, but Patrick didn't look up.

"Pssst!" I whispered loudly, but of course he didn't hear. I didn't dare call out to him, because others would have heard it too, and it would have ruined the mystery.

Patrick started back inside, heading to the door beneath the window. I had to let him know I was okay. Holding the roll out as far as I could, I let it drop.

Peering down below, I saw Patrick stop, stare at the toilet paper, then up toward the second floor.

Up here! Up here! I wanted to call. He looked down at the toilet paper again, then tipped his head way back and looked up. This time he saw me and stepped backward a foot or two. I held my finger to my lips, ducking back as another couple looked up at the same time, then peeped out again after they'd walked on. Patrick was grinning now. He gave me the OK sign and went on inside.

Now there were voices and laughter from below. The search party had begun. The sound of footsteps going up and down the stairs; voices calling out to each other from the next room.

It was another twenty minutes before the two men came back, and this time they had two more men with them, carrying a plywood box painted like a casket.

"I've got to lie in that?" I said.

"Only until we tap on the lid, then you push

open the top and crawl out. We'll take it from there. Thanks for being such a good sport and helping the plot along."

"But what *is* the plot?" I insisted. Even if I had no lines, I wanted to play the part.

"The story tonight is that the host has persuaded the guests that not only is one of their number missing, but that his criminally insane twin has escaped his quarters and is roaming the mansion. Edgar pretends to fear for the safety of the missing girl and has promised his guests that whoever finds her will get his dinner on the house. But all the while, Edgar and his brother, Allan, not deranged at all, have been quietly picking the pockets of their guests as they grope about looking for the missing girl—which is, of course, you."

"And when do I get to come back in?"

"Edgar has stolen you away himself and locked you in an upstairs room, supposedly. But unbeknownst to him and his thieving brother, two detectives have infiltrated the dinner party. They have rescued you, retrieved the bag of stolen wallets and jewelry, and at the critical moment—shortly after Edgar reports to his guests that he had no choice but to shoot his brother . . ."

A shot rang out from below.

"Our cue," the man noted, then continued, ". . . the detectives enter the room carrying a coffin—not of the brother, who faked his death, but of the missing girl, very much alive—and the bag of jewels."

It would have been a grade-D movie, and the plot would never have made it beyond fifth-grade English, but it was fun.

When we got downstairs, just outside the dining room, I climbed into the coffin and we listened as Edgar dramatically gave the account of finding his brother in an upstairs room, about to strangle the missing girl. There was a swell of recorded organ music, and the men carried me into the dining room, the lid of the coffin closed.

"What's this?" I heard the host exclaim. "This isn't part of the plot!"

Laughter from the audience, and I tried to hear Patrick's laughter in it.

There was more protracted conversation between Edgar and the detectives, and then I realized that someone was tapping repeatedly on the coffin. I rose up, hands folded over my chest, and climbed out of the coffin and onto the floor.

The detectives announced that the plan was foiled, that they had retrieved all the wallets and jewels, and different actors scattered among the guests cried out in fake surprise when pearls and money clips and wallets were returned to them. Everyone hooted and clapped as the host was led out of the room in handcuffs, protesting all the way.

Patrick and I laughed about it on the way home, and he was especially pleased that we got our dinner free, not because he had found me—no one had—but because I had played along.

"So was it worth the loss of my companionship?" I asked, glancing over at him as he drove back down Georgia Avenue.

"Oh, *nothing* could compensate me for that," he said, "but if I had to eat hoary beef again, I don't think I'd do it."

"Well, I had a good time," I said.

"So did I," said Patrick. And when we got up on the porch, he said we should end the evening with a flourish. At that, he swooped me up in his arms, bent me over backward, and gave me such a movie-star kiss that I expected us both to fall over, but we didn't.

And then he was gone and I was grinning. *Grinning*. It was not exactly the way I imagined our evening would end, but I think it erased forever the kiss on the forehead from Scott.

9

Moving On

I woke up smiling, thinking about that kiss. About the fact that the food was forgettable, the performance was awful, and yet we'd managed to have fun.

Snuggling down under my blanket, I wanted to imagine what it might have been like if I could have invited Patrick inside. If there had been *space* to squeeze him inside. If he could have sat down in Dad's armchair, me on his lap, Patrick's hand on my . . .

I heard voices coming from somewhere, the slam of a car or truck door, footsteps, more voices, and suddenly I remembered that this was the day we could move into our new addition.

I sprang out of bed and bounded to the bathroom before the workmen came upstairs. I was as excited as a kid at Christmas.

My first thought, of course, was that this

bathroom would be all mine now, except for the times Les spent the night. My second thought was that I could cozy up to a guy in the family room—Patrick or someone else—while Dad and Sylvia stayed back in the living room. I did a quick washup, tied my hair in a ponytail, brushed my teeth, and slipped on my old jeans and a T-shirt.

"Today's the day!" Sylvia said happily as she came up the stairs. "Just wanted to see if you were decent before I let the workmen come up."

"Bring 'em on!" I said. "I can't wait."

I made myself a piece of toast and trailed along after the burly workmen like a five-year-old. They started upstairs, untaping the thick blue wall of plastic that sealed off Dad and Sylvia's old bedroom. Yesterday we'd heard the sound of sweeping and vacuuming coming from the new addition, and now, foot by foot, the plastic was peeled away, exposing the windows of the bright new master bedroom, sunlight streaming through. There were the two doors to the walk-in closets and another door leading to the master bath, with its double-sink vanity and Jacuzzi tub.

I didn't even have to ask.

"Yes, Alice, you may use it whenever you like," Sylvia said, smiling as she studied my face.

"It's all beautiful!" I said. "How did you stand that old cramped bedroom for so long?"

"I wonder that myself," Dad said.

But the workmen were rolling up the blue plastic and heading downstairs, so I trotted along after them. They started at the wall between the kitchen and the hallway, and when the new cabinets came into view, then the new stainless steel sink, I had to be the first to go through, because beyond the kitchen was the family room, with its big stone fireplace all the way to the ceiling.

"I can fit *everyone* in this room!" I said, thinking about the newspaper staff, the GSA, stage crew, and whoever was left of the gang that used to gather at Mark Stedmeister's.

"I could invite the teachers from school!" said Sylvia.

"We could even hold the Melody Inn Christmas party here," said Dad.

But this wasn't all. There was a screened porch beyond the family room, and then, coming back inside, I entered the door that led to the new study, and a door from the study to the revamped dining room, and when the workmen pulled off the last of the plastic sheets, I was back in our old living room and then the hallway again. It was as though we had moved into a brand-new house, and I loved it.

There was no furniture yet for the family room or study. The workmen moved Dad and Sylvia's bedroom set into their new bedroom. They put the appliances back in the kitchen and disconnected the temporary sink they had hooked up in the living room. They moved the dining room table and chairs back where they belonged, and Dad's computer and table into the study.

"It'll be another couple weeks before we take care of all the small stuff, but you folks go ahead and put your things where you want them, and we'll work around you," the foreman said before the men left. And then it was just the three of us, exclaiming over each room, pointing out little details, opening cupboards, eager to put things back on shelves and in drawers, to spread out and *breathe* again. Annabelle moved cautiously through the rooms, sniffing at all the new scents, her tail straight up in the air.

Back upstairs, I moved all of Dad and Sylvia's clothes out of my room and into their new closets. Then I tackled the bathroom, helpfully taking all their stuff out of the medicine cabinet and from under the sinks and transferring it to their new bathroom. I moved their towels as well, and when I was done, I wiped off the shelves and rearranged my own shampoo and conditioner and cosmetics. Was I lucky or was I lucky?

We ordered pizza for dinner and ate it in lawn chairs we'd moved up from the basement into our new family room. It was hardly cold enough for a fire in the fireplace, but we built one anyway. I felt as though we were the richest people in the world, to have a stone fireplace that reached the ceiling.

"I can hardly believe it's finished," said Sylvia. "Oh, Ben, I'm so happy with the way it's turned out."

Dad put an arm around her on the aluminum love seat they were sharing. "So am I," he said. "How about a bearskin rug, right here by the fire?"

Sylvia's smile disappeared. "You don't mean that."

"Of course I mean it! A large brown rug. . . . No, maybe a polar bear skin—with the head and paws still attached. And a buck's head and antlers on the wall between the windows."

She knew he was teasing then, and we started to laugh. The doorbell rang, and I was still smiling when I went to answer.

"Patrick!" I couldn't believe I'd forgotten he might come by.

"Just your friendly neighborhood moving man!" he said. "Am I too late?"

"Not for pizza, you're not. We've still got a couple slices left," I said. "Come on in."

We gave him the official tour, and even

though Patrick's family has a bigger house than we do, even with our addition, Patrick said all the right things. He especially liked the fireplace.

We *didn't* exactly have everything moved, because when Patrick asked Dad if there was anything he could do, Dad asked if he'd move the boxes of books he'd left up in Lester's room, as well as Sylvia's three-drawer file cabinet.

After the fifth box of books, Patrick stripped down to his T-shirt. I was amazed at the broad range of his shoulders, the muscular back, the wide chest.

"Sure that's not too heavy for you?" Dad asked as Patrick lifted out one of the drawers of the file cabinet, holding Sylvia's records and lesson plans.

"Not any heavier than the mulch I've been unloading all week," Patrick said.

"That landscaping job obviously agrees with you, Patrick," Sylvia said.

"Yeah," Patrick said. "That's what all the girls say."

Dad and Sylvia went upstairs at last to organize their new closets, and Patrick and I had the family room to ourselves. We were sitting side by side on two aluminum chairs.

"Well, the *fire's* nice, anyway," he said, glancing over at me. "Can't say much for the chairs."

"Wait," I said.

I ran upstairs to my bedroom and lugged down the old beanbag chair I've had for as long as I can remember, plus all the pillows off my bed. We propped the pillows against the wall, put my beanbag chair in front of them. Then Patrick sank down in the chair and I sat on his lap, just as I had imagined. We turned out the lights and watched the fire.

And . . . little by little . . . memories, feelings came winging back. Some came at me sideways, sneaking in at an angle. Others came head-on, and still others came as a pair. The scent of his skin, the texture of his hair, the way he nestled his chin against my shoulder, stroked my side, just at the edge of my breast. I loved the way he pressed his lips against my cheek or my arm or my neck—not a kiss exactly, as though just touching me with his lips was all he needed.

I let myself be vulnerable. "It's nice to have you back," I said, trust overriding caution.

"Nice to be back," he whispered.

I didn't say it was nice to be a couple again, because—well, who knows?

Saturday morning, since I didn't have to go to the Melody Inn with Dad, I was working on a special article for *The Edge*. This year April 25 would be observed as the Day of Silence by Gay/Straight Alliances in high schools and colleges all over the country. But because it was new to our school, and because that date would coincide with the final weekend of our spring musical, we decided to hold our Day of Silence two weeks earlier, on Friday, April 11. To emphasize how gays and lesbians have had to keep their sexual orientation hidden, those of us in the GSA were going all day long wearing armbands and staying silent as a way of demonstrating what gays have had to do.

Since I was a member, Miss Ames had asked me to write an article explaining what it meant and how any student who wanted to show solidarity was welcome to join in. We didn't want kids to think that the GSA was some kind of cult or that we were using the silence as a way of not having to answer questions in class.

My final draft of the article was half done when Sylvia came to the door of my bedroom.

"Ben and I are going shopping for family room furniture," she said. "Do you want to come along and help choose?"

I looked up. "Well . . . sure!" I said. "I thought it was a done deal."

"We've only looked. Haven't decided on anything," she told me.

I changed my shirt, put on my shoes, and we were out the door.

"Saw some furniture we liked at Scan in Rockville," Dad said. "Let's swing by there first."

I sat happily in the backseat, thrilled to have been asked along. I had a new CD in my bag and would have loved to hear it again on the car player, but I wasn't going to press my luck. Traffic was awful and I didn't want to make Dad tense.

Somehow I knew when we walked into Scan, with its sleek modern furniture, that this was probably the place, and I was right. A rosewood desk for the study, bookcase to match, a lamp.

But when it came time to buy the couch and chairs for the family room, nothing really said *Comfortable* to me. Nothing said, *Welcome* or *Hanging out* or *Put up your feet.*

Dad and Sylvia studied my face.

"I don't know . . . ," I said.

"We don't have to buy everything from one store," said Sylvia. "Let's try Marlo's."

That store was huge. There were whole sets of furniture, whole room displays, one after another.

"Hey, look at this!" said Dad. He liked a high-backed sofa in tweed, with masculine-looking chairs. "Price is right," he said, checking the tags.

"Possibly," said Sylvia, which probably meant *Ugh.* "Let's keep looking."

Sylvia liked color, and she longingly fingered an Ultrasuede sofa in soft peach, with matching armchairs. It was okay, but . . . could I see myself hanging out with peach? I gave a little shrug.

"Well, there's more," Sylvia said, lingering a minute longer, and then we moved on.

The sofa that caught my eye was an L-shaped sectional that you could take apart and rearrange. It came with a huge ottoman on which at least four people could rest their feet, and the whole set was marine blue.

"Hey, what about *this*?" I said. "This is neat!"

Dad and Sylvia stopped to look at it. Their expressions were engraved in granite, and because I couldn't tell one way or the other how they felt, that should have told me something.

"Well, it's interesting," said Dad.

"I don't know about the color," said Sylvia. "We were sort of sticking to cinnamon or beige or something that would blend with—" She stopped. "It's certainly a possibility," she said.

I tried it out and sank down five inches. I leaned back and put my feet on the ottoman. "It's really comfortable," I told them.

A salesman standing by came over.

"Does this set come in any other colors?" Sylvia asked him.

"I'm afraid not. This is a one of a kind," he told her. "We got it from another store, half price."

Dad sat down on the sofa. He tried tipping his head, but the back wasn't high enough to support him.

And suddenly I realized that I would be out of the house in a year, away at college, but they would be in the house for a long time yet. The rest of their lives, maybe. Once I started college, I'd probably be home just for the summers, and after that I'd drop in only now and then, like Les.

"I'm willing to look around some more," I said, and saw the relief on their faces.

We ended up with an apricot-colored couch with thick cushions and a high back, along with two matching chairs and a rocker. Then we drove back to Scan and bought a perfectly gorgeous area rug to go with it, in apricot, ginger, and olive. And finally a new rug for my bedroom, in a sort of African print. I loved it.

We were so pleased with our shopping expedition that we went to Gifford's and ordered Swiss chocolate sundaes with Swiss chocolate sauce. When the clerk asked if we wanted whipped cream, nuts, and cherries, Dad said, "Why not?"

• • •

Molly called me on Monday and said she was having trouble finding costumes for Adelaide's chorus girls. Mr. Ellis had told her to get everything she possibly could free of charge from merchants who would be glad to have their companies or stores listed as sponsors in the program. Community service always got the attention of parents and teachers.

"He said we'd rent whatever we absolutely had to, but I'd love to get practically everything we need without having to pay a cent," she said.

"What don't you have yet?" I asked.

"Black net stockings and short sexy costumes that would look okay with a cat's ears and tail," said Molly.

"Oh, wow!" I said.

"I can buy cheap stockings on the Internet, but if we could find the right kind of costumes locally, they'd probably come with the stockings," said Molly.

"What sizes do you need?" I asked, and she read off the sizes of the girls who were playing Adelaide's "alley kittens" in the chorus, Pamela included.

"I'll see what I can do," I promised. I spent the evening looking through the Yellow Pages, then called Elizabeth.

Tuesday after school, Liz and I drove to a place just over the D.C. line called Nighttime Fantasies. They'd advertised "costumes for every taste and occasion." Liz insisted on wearing dark glasses when we parked and walked down the block, but when we got in front of the store window, I said, "Better take them off so you can see better. You don't want to miss this."

Elizabeth took off the glasses and looked at the display window. She stared for a minute and popped her glasses back on.

"I'm leaving," she said.

I laughed. "No, you're not. We got this far."

"But . . ." She was staring some more. "Do people really *use* this stuff? I mean, this part goes in, and that . . ."

"Don't ask," I said, but I was trying to figure the gadgets out too. Trying to figure out how couples climbed in bed with a bunch of sex toys and kept the mood while they figured out how to use them.

"Maybe they practice ahead of time," said Liz.

We went inside, and a little bell tinkled. A woman with obviously dyed red hair and a very low neckline got up from a stool behind a counter and put down the magazine she was reading. She smiled knowingly as we came in.

"May I help you?" she asked.

"Just looking," said Liz.

We were looking, all right. There were crotchless panties and curved appliances, about the size of a cell phone, "to increase feminine satisfaction." There were black leather hip-length boots, and whips and ostrich feather "ticklers," and condoms flavored raspberry, chocolate, and cinnamon. Oils to put in secret places, satin sheets, bras with no cups, navel jewels, penis enlargers, and racks of sexy nightwear, for him and for her.

"We're here from the high school newspaper *The Edge*," I said, and immediately the woman's expression changed. Her eyes grew cold, lips pressed into a straight line. I could tell that she thought we were going to do an exposé of students coming in to buy stuff, but when I told her what we wanted and what they were for, her eyes twinkled and she began to smile again.

"And my store will be included in the list of donors?" she asked.

"Absolutely," I said. "We'll send you two free tickets, and will include a program when we bring back your costumes, all dry-cleaned of course."

So who would have thought that someone's sexual fantasy was to be a kitten! We smiled all the way back to the car, a shopping bag in my hand. Wait till I told Molly that the program for *Guys and Dolls* would express our gratitude not only to Giant, CVS, the Mercy Mission, and the Department of Motor Vehicles, but to Nighttime Fantasies as well.

10

Promotion

All during spring break, I had worked really hard on that article about the Day of Silence. I found out how the first observance began. I described the way many gays and lesbians were ostracized, not only at school and by former friends, but in their own families. I wrote about methods people have used to try to change sexual orientation. Most of this I got from articles Mr. Morrison had given me, but I also interviewed some of the members of the GSA.

I think it was one of my best articles. I'd quoted Lori and Leslie on how it had been for them and recounted the time back in middle school when some girls cornered them in a restroom and kept taunting them with "Kiss her! Kiss her!" I ended the article by saying that the GSA wasn't trying to change anyone's sexual orientation; it existed to help people accept others' sexuality as much as to feel good about their own.

At the first staff meeting after spring break, I arrived early, and both Miss Ames and Scott read my piece and commented on it. Tony Osler just sat off to one side with a knowing smile, like, *Is that what's wrong with you, Alice? Why you wouldn't let me go all the way?* I know what Tony's thinking even when his lips are sealed.

"It's really excellent, Alice," Miss Ames said.

"It's great!" said Scott. "So what other ideas do you have for us?"

"Well . . . we do a lot of student interviews, polls and stuff," I said. "Why not do something called 'Teachers' Secrets'?"

"Whoa!" said Tony. "Report on who's sleeping with whom?"

I gave him a look. "No. I thought of asking fifteen or twenty teachers to tell us something about themselves that their students probably don't know—anything they want to share. See what we come up with."

Miss Ames smiled a little. "Could be interesting."

"We could start with you," said Scott, warming to the idea. "How about it?"

"We have to be sure we don't print anything

that's said off the record," she said. "But . . . well, let me think. I guess one thing students don't know about my past is that I once won a hot dog eating contest at the beach."

"*You?*" said the sophomore roving reporter. "You're so thin!"

"Well, thin girls have stomachs too." Miss Ames laughed.

"How many did you eat?" I asked.

"Eleven and a half. They almost disqualified me because I threw up before they announced the winner, but the judge said I got it all down, and that's what counts."

Everybody cheered.

Jacki Severn breezed in just then and apologized for being late, but she said she had just got this great idea for the next issue:

"It's our first issue in April—you know, April showers and stuff. I remembered this photo from last year when there was all that rain and the parking lot flooded. Remember? Mom took this picture when she came to pick me up. . . ." And Jacki pulled out a picture of herself, laughing as she waded ankle-deep in water, holding her books over her head. A couple of friends were behind her, but obviously, Jacki was the main attraction. "I thought we could title it 'April! Will It Happen

Again?' And I'll interview other kids to see how they got home that day."

Scott looked at the picture, smiled a little, and passed it on. "I don't know, Jacki. It's old news. We should have used it last year," he said.

"All the more reason to use it now!" Jacki said emphatically. She always speaks louder when she wants to make a point. "It would make a great story! One of the teachers said that the water came up so fast that the physics teacher was stranded at the end of the parking lot!"

"Our freshman class wasn't even here last year," said Miss Ames. "It wouldn't mean much to them."

"It doesn't make any difference!" Jacki argued. "The tie-in is April! Spring! Rain! I think it would get a lot of attention on the front page."

"Well, that's not going to happen," said Scott. "The school board's ruling on sex ed is the top story. And the bottom half of the first page will be the Day of Silence."

Jacki stared incredulously around the room. "Day of *Silence*? The gay thing? That doesn't have to be front page, for God's sake! It's not like it affects the whole school."

"Well, perhaps it should," said Miss Ames. "That's our point."

"I thought *I* was the features editor!" Jacki fumed.

Everyone was staring now. Sam Mayer had come in with the sports photos for the next edition, and he immediately sat down on a desk near the door, out of the line of fire.

"Jacki, we discussed the Day of Silence piece at the last meeting, and you didn't say a word about a feature on rain, much less a photo," said Scott.

"Well, *I* thought a newspaper could be spontaneous!" cried Jacki. "*I* thought we were supposed to be current, and what could be more current than the month of the year! If we have a big rain between now and next week when the paper comes out, we'll be right on top of the news."

Tony had been reading the Metro section of the *Washington Post*, and he turned to the weather report on the back page. "Five-day forecast," he said aloud. "Fair and breezy."

"Well, I won't insist on the front page, but there's no way I'm going to settle for putting my feature on the *last* page," said Jacki.

"I've got the basketball scores, and Sam's got photos," said Tony. "Those have to go somewhere."

"What about news from the roving reporters?" asked another guy.

"And we're printing the cast for *Guys and Dolls*. We've got to start publicizing that," said Scott.

"Jacki, since this is the first year we've had a GSA in our school, it's important that students understand its purpose," Miss Ames explained. "And because we're holding our Day of Silence two weeks before the national observance, it's especially important that this feature make the coming issue."

"Then we can take out something else!" Jacki said hotly. "If we put my feature off, April will be half over by the time it comes out."

"Then I'm sorry," Miss Ames said, "but there just isn't room for it."

I hadn't said a word. I wasn't even certain I was breathing. Jacki's cheeks flamed. I'd never seen those large red blotches on her face before, but there they were, as though she'd been out in the wind.

"In that case, I quit!" she said, and threw down the features editor's notebook. Papers sailed across the floor. She strode past me, her arm brushing mine, and plowed on out the door, almost knocking down the freshman roving reporter who was just coming in.

For a moment no one spoke.

"Wow!" said Tony finally.

Scott sucked in his breath. "Whew!"

"Oh, she'll get over it," said Sam, ever the conciliator.

But Miss Ames quietly picked up the notebook, and the rest of us began gathering up the scattered pages.

"Alice," Miss Ames said, "would you be features editor for the rest of the year?" She looked at Scott. "Is that okay with you?"

"More than okay," he answered.

I didn't know what to say. My God, taking over for Jacki! She'd kill me.

"Sure," I said.

"She left the room like a tornado!" I told Sylvia later when we were sharing a bagel in the kitchen. We both like ours lightly toasted. She uses butter, I like cream cheese.

"Sure sounds like an overreaction to me. Maybe she thought they'd go after her and beg her to come back," said Sylvia.

"Fat chance," I said. "If I had to describe the atmosphere after she left, I'd call it relief. But, Sylvia, she'll *hate* me! She never did like me very much."

"Do you care?" asked Sylvia. "She's a senior, you said. Do you have any classes with her?"

"No. . . ."

"She probably expects the paper to fall apart if she's not on it. Prove that it won't. Do you have any plans for the next issue?"

"That's all wrapped up. But I was thinking about the next few issues on my way home. Like, now that the school year's almost over, maybe the freshman roving reporter could do a little piece on fears that freshmen have when they start high school, and how things really turned out."

"Possibility," said Sylvia.

"Or maybe that would be better for fall," I went on. "We could also interview Molly on the ingenious ways she's getting all the props for *Guys and Dolls*. We wouldn't even have to say she's doing all this from home. Help her feel more connected to school."

"I like that idea," said Sylvia.

"And we could also assign the senior roving reporter to do an article on what kids who aren't going to college are going to do—like travel or help out at home or get a job. . . ."

"You're full of ideas, you know it?" Sylvia said. "And you know why I think you'll make a better features editor than Jacki? Because your focus is on broadening the scope of the paper, getting other kids involved, not just on what kind of article you could fashion around yourself."

"Thanks," I said, pleased.

"But *also*," Sylvia added, "I've read the features you've written, and you're not afraid to let your emotions show. It helps the reader connect with you."

I wondered if she knew what she was saying— if she'd forgotten that fight we had last November over her car. I'd let my emotions show then, all right—the worst ones. I'd wondered then if Sylvia and I would ever be friends again. And obviously, we were.

"It took me a while to learn that," she said.

"Learn what?"

"To express my feelings. My family was sort of formal when I was growing up. Reserved, I mean. Consequently, when anyone was really angry or sad, it was kind of scary."

"How . . . *did* you act when you were angry?" I asked.

"When we had arguments, it was more like a debate society. I even thought I was more mature than other girls simply because I could hold in my feelings. What a mistake!"

"Really?"

She nodded. "It was Mom's funeral that turned me around. Dad didn't cry, so I didn't. When I felt tears welling up, I learned to stop them before my eyes brimmed over. And everyone commented on how brave I was, how well I held up." Sylvia shook her head. "For months after that, I'd do my crying in private, and I never allowed myself to cry in front of friends. And then I began to wonder: Why is this good? Why is it important? Why do I have to be a 'real trouper,' as the neighbors called me?

"And then, when Dad died—and I'll always believe it was from all the sorrow he'd kept inside—I sort of went to pieces. I cried all over the place. At school, at the mall. . . . I cried out of grief and anger both, that Dad had held his feelings in and passed that legacy on to me and my sister and brother."

I thought about that awhile. "Can you really die of a broken heart?"

"A lot less likely if you can share your feelings with someone. It's amazing, really, what a good listener can do—no solutions necessary." She blinked suddenly. "How did we get started on this?"

"You were talking about expressing emotion."

"Right. And because you can express yours, you're going to be a good features editor, I can tell."

"It's only for the next couple of months," I told her.

● ● ●

But it wasn't. When the first April issue came out with my article about the meaning of the Day of Silence, the principal told Miss Ames that it was one of our best.

"Alice," she said, "I don't usually appoint the new staff until fall, but you've already got your feet wet as features editor. If you plan on being on the newspaper next year, I'd like to keep you in that spot."

"I'd love it!" I said, thrilled, and everyone came over to give me a hug, Scott and Sam and Don and Tony included.

Jacki Severn had passed by me that morning as I was delivering my bundle of papers to homerooms, and her glare was as cold as the frost on a soda can.

By lunchtime some of her choice phrases were making the rounds: "They don't recognize the importance of a good photo on the front page" and "Alice as features editor is a laugh and a half."

A half hour before school let out that day, the office made an announcement: "We're sorry for the interruption, but due to an electronic glitch, the yearbook needs new photos of the following: the senior class officers, the Sadie Hawkins Day dance committee, and the newspaper staff for *The Edge*. As you know, the deadline for the yearbook has passed, but we're holding up production until we get these three photos. Will all students who belong in those photos please report to the auditorium immediately after the close of school. . . ."

I needed a haircut and wished I'd worn a different shirt. I especially wished my braces were off. But after the last bell I went down to the auditorium, where the photographer was already lining up the dance committee.

The senior class officers were sitting on the steps of the stage eating doughnuts, and members of the newspaper staff were milling around at the back of the auditorium.

"I hope he makes this quick, because I'm supposed to drive my brother to the dentist," Scott said, glancing at his watch.

"I'll ask if he can take our picture next," Miss Ames said. "I've got an appointment too."

At that very moment Jacki Severn came through the double doors and smiled as though we were her best and only friends.

"Miss Ames," she said, in a voice as phony as it was poignant, "I was really having a bad day last Wednesday, and I apologize. I still think I had a good idea, but . . . well, I can't win them all. So anyway, I want to be a good sport. I heard the

announcement about a new photo, so I'm report-
ing for duty."

No one said a word—just looked toward
Miss Ames.

"Oh, I'm sorry, Jacki," the teacher said. "But
Alice is now features editor, so you're excused.
Thanks for coming by."

Jacki blanched. "There are only two months
left of school," she said. "I've been features editor
for almost the whole year!"

Miss Ames nodded. "Until last Wednesday.
But you resigned, and I've appointed Alice."

Jacki looked almost numb with astonish-
ment. "But I'm a senior! And this is *my* yearbook,
not Alice's!"

"I know, and that's really a shame. But a
newspaper can't run with unpredictable people
on the staff. If you'd like to be listed as co-editor
of features, along with Alice, you may stay for the
photo if you like."

"But I . . ." Jacki looked at her pleadingly. "I've
already listed this on my college applications! I'll
be using it on my resume when I look for a job! I
didn't say I was a co-editor."

"That's fine, Jacki. You can tell anyone you
like that you were a member of the staff, and you
were. But you can't be listed any other way than

co-editor for the photo, because you're no longer features editor."

I think that Jacki was on the verge of throwing her whole armful of books on the floor, and she probably does that at home, who knows? But she must have thought better of it, because she gave us all a hateful look, spun round, and marched back through the double doors, thundering on.

Miss Ames said nothing. The rest of us gave each other secret smiles as we followed her down the aisle and tried to look professional as the photographer lined us up for the picture.

I wasn't sure how the photo would come out, but I was standing sleeve to sleeve between Scott and Tony, and Don and Sam were on either side of them, along with the roving reporters and our layout coordinator. I was pleased as anything when Miss Ames read off my part of the caption: "Alice McKinley, Features Editor and Junior Class Roving Reporter."

Sometimes the bad guys *don't* win!

11

The Performing Arts

Pamela was getting impossible. She sang every chance she got. It wasn't like she was showing off. She was just trying to memorize Adelaide's songs. All of Adelaide's lines. She had to memorize the songs the chorus sang as well, plus do her homework and still squeeze time out of all that for her boyfriend.

"I *almost* wish she hadn't gotten a part," Tim said as we sat together in the auditorium after school, watching another rehearsal. "Almost, but not quite. I'm glad for her, sure, but it's like she's turned into this . . . robot. Press a button and she sings. Press another and she eats. Press another and she—"

"Never mind," I said quickly. "It'll all be over in three more weeks."

There had been rehearsals every day, often well into the evening. Since I'd volunteered to

THE PERFORMING ARTS • 155

help paint some of the sets, most of my work would be done ahead of time. I didn't have to adjust the lighting or tweak the sound. Molly had enlisted so many volunteers—*every*one wanted to help Molly—that the props were well taken care of, so some of the time I was able to go home pretty early while Pamela had another hour or two of practice yet to go.

If Tim hadn't been at a restaurant celebrating his mom's birthday on Saturday, I don't know when we would have had Pamela to ourselves. The minute Gwen found out she had a free Saturday night, she invited Pamela, Liz, and me to sleep over.

"I really should be studying for that French test," Pamela told me as I drove to Gwen's in Dad's car, Liz in the backseat.

"Pam, you've got to relax a little! You're so tight, you're going to snap a string!" Liz told her. "You're starting to get lines on your forehead."

Pamela reached for her bag and pulled out a mirror, trying to see herself in the dark interior of the car. When we got to the Wheelers', we told Gwen not to let her in until she smiled, and Pamela finally got the message.

Gwen's mom had made paella and a salad, and we heaped our plates with shrimp and sausage and mussels and took over the family room.

Mrs. Wheeler stood in the doorway in jeans and a T-shirt. She works at the Justice Department and puts in long hours on weekdays—sometimes Saturdays, too—so I don't usually see her in anything but a suit.

"There's some mint chocolate chip in the freezer, but I can only guarantee it till eleven or so, when the guys get home," she said. "They went to a movie."

"Great paella!" I told her. "Seconds?"

"As long as it lasts," she said, laughing. "When those boys get home, everything that's not nailed down gets devoured. Be careful they don't fall over you. Bill's idea of indoor lighting is to turn on the TV."

Gwen's grandmother—"Granny," Gwen calls her—was watching TV in her own little apartment at the back of the house, and we took some ice cream in to her before we settled down for the evening.

"You remember my friends?" Gwen asked her. "Elizabeth, Pamela, and Alice?"

Granny looked up from the *TV Guide* for a moment, pointed to the screen, and said, "*That* program should never be on TV. I don't like it."

On the screen a drunken couple had just taken off in a car they had hijacked.

"Then don't watch it, Granny. Turn it off," said Gwen.

"If I turn it off, someone else will watch it," said the little woman in the pink sweater and the glasses at the end of her nose. She studied us over the rims. "You girls don't watch this, do you?"

"What is it?" asked Liz.

Granny looked at the *TV Guide* again. *"Prime Crime,"* she said. "If you run out of bad things to do, you just turn on this program. I never saw such trash."

Gwen picked up the remote and changed the channel, but Granny grabbed for it. "It's only the ending that's good," she said. "The villains always get it in the end, but what they've been doing in the meantime is something we don't need to know a thing about."

Gwen leaned down and kissed her on the cheek as she set the ice cream on the little stand beside her. "Well, if you insist on watching it, don't come crying to me if you have nightmares," she teased.

Granny thought that over for a moment or two, then smiled. "Nice to meet you, girls," she said, wanting to get back to her program. "And, Gwen, say a prayer for your Uncle Albert. He's got himself a new car, and you know how he drives."

We were smiling too as we left Granny's apartment.

We hunkered back down in the family room with our ice cream, and the first hour was filled with gossip—who went where and said what—then boyfriend biz, mostly about Tim. I sort of wanted to keep my feelings about Patrick to myself for a while, and though Liz had gone out with a couple guys since the Sadie Hawkins dance, she didn't have a boyfriend, and Gwen had sworn off guys till summer.

"The problem," Gwen said, "is that I want a guy around when it's convenient for me, and I *don't* want him around when I'm studying or doing family stuff. No guy's going to put up with that."

"A guy who's as serious as you are, maybe," I told her.

"Gwen, if you could choose any guy you wanted, what would he be like?" Liz asked.

"Hmmm." Gwen leaned back against the couch, palms resting beside her on the rug. "He would absolutely have to have a goal. I wouldn't want any guy who doesn't have a picture of where he wants to be ten years from now."

"Really?" said Pamela. "I want to be on Broadway, but that doesn't mean I'll get there."

"I'm not interested in guys who are content

to just let life happen," said Gwen. "I want a guy with plans."

"Then you should be dating Patrick," I said.

"Don't think I haven't considered it," she said, and laughed.

I was curious. "Did he ever ask you out?"

"No, but I was tempted to ask *him* out a time or two. Back when you were going out with Sam. But Patrick was never around long enough to ask, it seemed. Dad thinks I ought to stick to guys my own race—less hassle—while Mom says go with your heart. But don't worry." She nudged me. "Everyone knows that Patrick belongs to you."

"What do you mean, everyone knows?" I asked. "He was going with Marcie for a while, remember? And with Penny? What's this 'he belongs to me' business?"

Gwen took another swallow of her Pepsi to hide a smile. "Oh, it's just that he has 'Alice' engraved on his forehead or something. Anyway . . ." She got up. "Let's do something different." There was a computer at one end of the family room, and she slipped in a software program that invited you to sing along to an accompaniment—words on the screen—then it would rate your performance. If you got a good score, you'd hear applause; the higher the score, the louder the applause. If you bombed, you'd get boos.

"Let's each try it," said Pamela, adding, "Not you, Alice. You're excused."

I was grateful for that, because they know I can't sing. But it was a blast listening to the three of them. Gwen went first. She chose country music. The guitar accompaniment played "She's Stolen My Man," and Gwen was awful. She's got a good voice—she sings with her church choir—but this time she gave the words a nasal twang and let her voice slide from note to note till we were hooting with laughter. She also purposely sang off-key, Pamela told me. I wouldn't know. Pamela says that's even more difficult to do than singing the right way. Gwen got a chorus of boos at the end, and that encouraged Liz to do a love song to violins. She put a lot of drama into it and got a good score, so we clapped and cheered along with the canned applause.

Finally Pamela got up to sing one of Adelaide's songs, "Pet Me, Poppa," and she did it up royally, the original sex kitten. We were all really into it by now, and we were shouting and cheering as she moved suggestively about the floor. Then she got down on her hands and knees, mewing like a cat, wiggling her hind end, and suddenly, out in the hall, we heard a male voice say, "What *is* it?" And one of Gwen's brothers walked in.

Pamela rolled herself into a ball of embar-rassment and wouldn't uncurl even though the song was over and the computer audience was cheering.

"Hey, Jerry!" Gwen laughed. "I want you to meet Adelaide. Adelaide, this is my brother Jerome."

And then Pamela, with the Brooklyn accent that only she can imitate, uncoiled herself, held out one limp hand, fingers down, as though offer-ing it to be kissed, and said, "Hello, big guiiy. Pleased t'meetcha."

Jerry laughed.

"Where's Bill?" Gwen asked.

"Deena came along, so he's with her," said Jerry. Both of Gwen's brothers are in college, though they're not as old as Lester. "Anything left from dinner?"

"Paella for one," Gwen said, and Jerry disap-peared.

Gwen's folks had gone to bed, so we settled down about midnight and got into our sleeping bags. Pam was the first one asleep. She's a noisy sleeper and hates it when we tell her she snores. I could tell that Gwen fell asleep next, because I could hear her slow, steady breathing a few feet away from me.

I lay there feeling a little sad that I couldn't

sing. It must have been fun hamming it up like that. Performing in front of your friends. I've missed some good times because of it— Christmas carols, joining in on "Happy Birthday," high school musicals, chorus. . . . The thing is, I'm so bad, so tone-deaf, I can't even tell the difference. I'd get a chorus of boos, but it wouldn't be funny.

My mind wandered back to the early embarrassment in grade school when I sang and was terrible but didn't know it. Kids stared at me at parties when the birthday song came around, and a music teacher once tried to figure out who was ruining "America the Beautiful."

I was on the verge of sleep when I heard soft voices coming from the hallway and the almost imperceptible close of a door.

My eyes popped open, and I remembered I was on the floor of the Wheelers' family room. Somebody was coming in. Any minute the light would come on, and I braced myself.

The murmurs continued, but there was no light.

"They don't know I'm here, Bill."

"So? I'm not going to wake them up to tell them."

"What if your dad comes down?"

"He won't. He sleeps like the dead."

"Your mom?"

"I'll turn on the TV. So we're watching TV. . . ."

A girl's giggle. "At one in the morning? What are we supposed to be watching?"

"The Weather Channel?"

More giggles. Murmurs.

Omigod! I thought. Bill was here with his girlfriend, and any second now I was going to get a foot in the face.

I coughed.

"What . . . ?" Bill's voice.

"Somebody's here!" The girl's frantic whisper.

"Mom?" Bill said tentatively.

I lowered my voice. "Go to bed," I said.

Silence.

"Bill! Your mom's on the sofa! Come *on*! Let's go!"

"Uh . . . I'm just taking Deena home," said Bill.

"Good," I answered.

There were hurried footsteps in the hallway. The soft opening and closing of the front door. Then I heard Liz's giggle from the other side of me.

"Alice, you were great!" she said. We rolled into each other, suppressing our laughter, and didn't tell the others till morning.

When we went in for breakfast around eleven, Mr. Wheeler was in his robe scrambling eggs for us.

"Your mother upset with me or something?" he asked Gwen as he set a plate of sausages on the table.

"You're asking *me*?" Gwen said. "Not that I know of."

"Well, I passed Bill in the hall this morning, and he murmured something about her sleeping on the couch last night. I thought she was in bed with me the whole time."

It was all we could do to keep our faces straight.

"Guess you'll have to talk that over with Mom," Gwen said.

On Monday, long-awaited Monday, after a year and a half of waiting for this Monday, I went to the orthodontist after school, and he removed my braces.

Eighteen months of Metal Mouth. Five hundred and forty days of catching spinach, corn, chicken—every edible thing—in my braces, of feeling that pull on my teeth, the soreness of my gums, the intrusion of wire when I kissed.

"Now," said Dr. Wiley when the last wire was removed, "look at that smile!" He handed me a mirror.

I grinned like the Cheshire cat, but to tell the truth, I didn't see that much of a difference. A straighter tooth here, maybe. A little less space between teeth there. But he said I now had a healthier mouth, a perfect alignment, a better bite, and my teeth could grow as God intended. And I wondered why God didn't make them grow right in the first place. But the orthodontist was happy, so I was happy. And I half regretted some of the remarks I'd made to him when I was most miserable. I especially regretted bleeding on his chair once during my period.

"Now, here's the thing," he told me, and his face was serious. "You *must* wear your retainer at least twelve hours a day, Alice, or your teeth will grow back like they used to be. Wear it at night, wear it at school, but you can take it out when you eat and for special occasions."

That's really all I wanted to hear—that I didn't have to wear my retainer to the prom.

"Gorgeous!" Sylvia told me when I got home. "Now you can do a full frontal smile."

I gave my full frontal smile to everyone I met the next day. I laughed at every joke, ran my tongue over my teeth for emphasis, ate an apple, and only one person noticed.

"What's so funny?" Patrick asked when he caught me grinning uncontrollably, and I guessed then that it was time to stop.

12

911

On April 11 the GSA had members stationed at all the school entrances to pass out armbands to anyone who wanted to show support for gays and lesbians to be who they are without having to hide it. There were also printed sheets explaining what the Day of Silence was all about in case anyone had missed my article. A few of the kids in the GSA wore tape over their mouths to emphasize their presence.

It was sort of a relief to go all day without talking, I discovered. Gwen wore an armband, but neither Liz nor Pamela took one, I noticed. I didn't ask them about it, but Pamela volunteered that it might be confusing to friends who knew she was going out with Tim. Liz simply said that if she couldn't answer questions in class, it might affect her grades. I guess all of us can think of excuses when we don't want to do something, but I know that this was an issue they would have to decide on personally; the GSA wasn't out to change people's minds with a wrench.

The teachers noticed which of us were wearing armbands and didn't ask us questions, and at lunch a bunch of GSA members sat together, so we wouldn't be tempted to talk to other friends.

What would it be like, I'd asked in my article, to have a secret so basic about who you really are and to feel you had to hide that part of yourself? What if I felt like a fraud, a phony? That I was pretending to be something I wasn't? What if I suddenly found myself on a planet where lesbians were the norm, and everyone kept trying to hook me up with a girl? How would I feel?

Most of the kids got it, I think. A couple of the guys who wore tape over their mouths got grins and a few jeers, but several people gave me the thumbs-up sign in the halls because of my article, and I found a note in my locker saying it was a good piece.

There was a little "breaking of silence" ceremony at the end of the day in the auditorium. Probably half the kids ditched and went to Ben & Jerry's, but the other half listened to Mr. Morrison explain how this would be an annual observance at our school, how it was intended to end bullying and harassment of gay students. He thanked us for participating and said that we were part of a national movement to send the message that hate would not be tolerated.

I looked forward to talking again when I got home, and the first conversation I had was with Aunt Sally, who called to ask if we had moved into our new addition yet. I described the rooms in detail.

"They sound lovely! I'll bet you're almost too busy to enjoy them, though, with all those extra things going on at school," she said.

"But guess what?" I told her. "I'm the new features editor for our school paper!" And I explained how Jacki Severn had quit and how Miss Ames wouldn't take her back. "The features editor plans the more in-depth articles we publish in each issue," I said.

"Features editor! Think of it!" said Aunt Sally. "Oh, your mother would have been so proud of you, dear! Those features are the best part of any newspaper! Of course, some features go a little deeper than they have to, but then, that's what newspapers do, I guess."

"Well, if you have any good ideas, let me know," I said.

"Why, I've got a good idea already," Aunt Sally said. "I think that every newspaper should have a column called 'The Answer Woman,' and that could be you."

I didn't know how to tell her that columns weren't considered features and that the last thing anyone would call me, least of all myself, was "The Answer Woman."

"Um . . . what do you mean?" I asked.

"Anybody could write in and ask a question; the Answer Woman would research it, and then she'd answer in the next issue," Aunt Sally explained. "And these would have to be the kinds of answers you couldn't always find on the Internet."

"Like what?" I asked.

"Like why is it that you can buy canned apricots with seeds only if they're peeled? If you want them unpeeled, they're cut in half and missing the seeds, and seeds give them flavor," Aunt Sally said.

"Huh?" I said.

"Why do you never see dead rabbits in the street? That's another question. You see dead squirrels, but when did you ever see a run-over rabbit?"

"Well, I . . ."

"And speaking of squirrels, did you ever see a baby squirrel? You see baby rabbits hopping through the tiger lilies in your yard, but when did you ever see a tiny squirrel skittering down a tree? Never."

She was right about that.

"Why can you say 'A girl whose clothes . . . ,' but you can't say 'A house whose windows . . .'? Did an English teacher ever explain why there's no word like 'whose' for an inanimate object? And don't get me started on sex. . . ."

"I wasn't about to," I murmured.

"Here's the question: Why do the parts of your body you make love with—well, not you, Alice, I mean married people's parts—have to be down *there*, for goodness' sake, right between those other parts we don't even *talk* about?"

"Well, the last time I looked, mine were down there too," I said.

"But *why*?" said Aunt Sally. "Why couldn't they be somewhere else . . . between the shoulder blades, maybe? Think how much neater it would be!"

I tried to imagine a man and woman rubbing their backs together.

"I don't know, Aunt Sally. Just doesn't do it for me, I guess. But I could do a feature story on *you* sometime," I told her.

Lester came over Sunday when we were sitting out on our new screened porch behind the family room. It was April at its best—birds everywhere, scouting out their territory—and Sylvia was talking about putting a bird feeder and bath out in the backyard . . . well, what was left of it, now that we'd put in the new addition. The air was balmy, breezy, totally perfect.

We heard a car door slam out front and, a little later, footsteps coming through the kitchen.

"Lester, I'll bet," Dad said, smiling.

We hadn't seen Les for several weeks and were sure he'd have come by when the renovations were complete. But his master's coursework wasn't over until the second week of April, so we knew he was too busy earlier this month to take time off.

"Anybody home?" Les called.

"Hey, Les!" Dad called. "Out here!"

I jumped up and ran inside. "Isn't this gorgeous?"

Lester walked into the family room. "Wow!" he said, looking around. "The Porta-John's gone! There's sod on the front yard! I can't believe it's finished!"

"Believe it," said Sylvia, coming in to give him a hug. "We're just loving this house, Lester. Come see the porch."

I followed him around like a puppy as we gave him a tour, wanting to see his reaction to everything.

"Now I wish we'd done it sooner," Dad told him. "All this space!"

"The fireplace! The windows! Man, oh, man!" Les said, then stepped out on the porch to look around there.

We moved from room to room, back to the hallway again and on upstairs. Lester gave a breathy whistle at each stop. "Fantastic job!" he said. "Great colors! If we'd had this addition when I was back in high school, think how I could have impressed the girls."

"Not up here in our bedroom, I hope," Dad said.

"And I don't have to share the bathroom with anyone, Lester!" I said, scrunching up my face at him. "Just think! The whole medicine cabinet! The entire countertop, just for me and my stuff!"

"Didn't I tell you I was moving back home for the summer?" he asked, and then, when all three of us looked at him in dismay, he burst out laughing.

We went downstairs again and sat around the table in our newly expanded kitchen. The coffee-pot was still plugged in from breakfast, and Sylvia brought out a plate of lemon bars. As Dad set cups on the table, he asked, "So how are things with you, Les? Everything squared away?"

When Lester didn't answer immediately, just

reached for the sugar, I could tell somehow that the news wasn't good.

"Well, could be better," he said. "I just found out that I can't present my thesis by the eleventh."

"Oh, Les!" said Sylvia. "What a disappointment for you!"

"They found something that major?" asked Dad.

"Afraid so. One of the philosophers I'm working on just had a new book come out that says pretty much exactly what I'm arguing."

"But does this invalidate your entire thesis?" Dad wanted to know.

"No, in a way, it's reassuring, but now I need to clarify exactly how my view is different from his and contributes something new to the debate. And it does, actually, but I haven't emphasized that as much, and an entire section needs an overhaul. I'm wiped out. I need a break."

Since I didn't understand much of anything they were talking about—and because his thesis had something to do with utilitarianism, I remembered that much—I just sat and tried to read their faces.

"So what's the plan?" asked Sylvia.

"I'll graduate in December, not May. Not what I'd hoped, but at least I know what I have to do," Lester said.

I'm embarrassed to say that my first thought was for myself. I'd already bought his graduation present—a beautiful expensive pen that looked like green marble and wrote so effortlessly that you hardly felt it touch the paper. And I'd found a funny little wire figure of a graduate in cap and gown, holding a diploma in one hand, a beer stein in the other. I'd even found a card! In fact, I'd imagined myself at his graduation ceremony yelling *Go, Les!* when he crossed the stage!

Graduation in December? The month reserved for Christmas? It just didn't compute.

Dad was concerned about finances. "Will your fellowship cover the next six months, Les?"

"Well, there is *some* good news," Lester said, putting down his cup and smiling a little. "The fellowship ends in June, but I've been hired to work in the admissions office full-time—just a low-level job, but it'll buy the food and gas and haircuts till I get my degree."

"Full-time?" I asked, because, as far as I knew, Les has never worked full-time in his life.

"Yeah. Hard to imagine, isn't it?" he joked.

"Well, it'll all turn out, Les," Sylvia said.

"And I sure can't complain about my living arrangements," said Les.

The windows were open all over the house, and a light breeze blew my paper napkin off the table. A lawn mower was going somewhere down the street, and off in the distance a siren sounded, seeming to grow louder. As it grew louder still, we paused in our conversation, expecting it to wane as it passed by on Georgia Avenue, but instead, it became earsplitting, with a honking and urgency that made us get up from the table. It sounded as though it were going to come right through the house.

I ran to the front door.

"It's Elizabeth's!" I yelled. "The fire truck's stopped right in front of their house!"

A second truck followed the first. We rushed outside. Smoke was coming out their opened front door. Mr. Price was standing on the porch, directing the firefighters inside. Mrs. Price was out on the lawn with Nathan, who pointed excitedly at a rescue vehicle just rounding the corner. Elizabeth stood a few feet away, her eyes huge, hand over her mouth.

Already one fireman was running up the steps to the porch with an ax, and a second was uncoiling the long hose and dragging it to the hydrant two doors down.

We carefully made our way across the street, as neighbors gathered on porches and sidewalks.

"Janet," Dad said, going up to Mrs. Price. "Is there any way we can help?"

"Oh, I don't know!" she said. "Isn't this *something*? We're not even sure where it's coming from. We started smelling smoke, and when Fred opened the basement door, it just rolled out! We can't tell what's on fire, and the dispatcher told us to get out of the house."

I looked at Liz and wondered if she was going to throw up. Her face was pale.

There was the sound of crashing glass, and immediately smoke came pouring out of a basement window.

I put one arm around her. "Don't worry," I said. "They'll have it under control in a minute."

"I was in the basement just ten minutes ago!" she said.

"Well, the firemen know what to look for," I told her.

An ambulance pulled up.

"No pets in there, are there?" Lester asked, coming over. Liz shook her head.

Nathan was jumping up and down. "Will they put up the ladder?" he kept asking. "I want to see them put up the ladder!" He tugged at his mother's hand.

"Nathan, *stop* it!" Mrs. Price said.

Sylvia came over and took Nathan's hand. "Here, Nathan. Let's go get a better look at that ladder," she said, and Mrs. Price gratefully turned him over to her care.

There seemed to be a lot of coming and going. We couldn't hear any more crashing of glass or banging. One fireman stood by the fire hydrant, waiting for an order to attach the hose. But the minutes ticked by, and the man who had run up the steps with an ax was replaced by a man with a clipboard. More discussion on the front porch with Elizabeth's dad.

Liz turned away, biting her bottom lip.

Finally the fireman on the porch gave a "roll-'em-up" sign to the man at the hydrant, who dragged the hose back to the truck.

"Oh, thank goodness!" Mrs. Price said. "They must have found the trouble. I'm afraid to look inside."

"Most likely smoke damage, but nothing major, I'll bet," said Les.

The smoke coming out the front door had stopped entirely, and smoke from the basement was growing weaker.

"I just can't imagine what it could have been!" Mrs. Price went on. "Elizabeth was doing the laundry for me, but we haven't had any trouble with the washer and dryer before."

The firemen were putting things away. The ambulance drove off. So did the rescue truck.

The first fireman came down the steps and across the lawn toward us. Perhaps, because I still had one arm around Liz, he thought we were part of the family.

"Everything's under control, ma'am," he said to Liz's mom. "You had a fire in the dryer, and I'm afraid you'll need a new one. But it only scorched the wall. Maybe have to scrub down a room or two upstairs."

"But what caused it?" Mrs. Price asked. "I cleaned out the lint trap only last week."

"Think it was this," the man said, reaching into the big pocket of his yellow fireproof jacket and handing something charred and black to Elizabeth's mom.

"What is it?" she said, and then, slowly pulling it apart, she stared down at the remains of a bra.

Liz's face turned pink with embarrassment. Her Stupefyin' Jones push-up bra!

"Probably shouldn't put those things in the dryer. Anything with rubber padding's likely to overheat," the fireman said. And with a quick nod to Dad, he walked back to the truck.

Mrs. Price looked at Elizabeth. "Whose *is* this?" she asked. Then she saw Elizabeth's embarrassment, and crumpled it up in her hand as Dad and Lester turned discreetly away.

"I got it at a costume shop," Liz said miserably. "It was just a cheap thing, but I've been wearing it a little. . . ."

Neighbors were coming over now to talk with Mrs. Price.

"What happened?" they asked. And Les, as usual, came to the rescue.

"Just a stuffed toy that caught fire in the dryer," he told them.

Mrs. Price nodded gratefully. "Some things just weren't meant to be washed," she said.

Les and Dad and Sylvia went inside with the Prices to look at the damage, but Liz and I sat down on the porch steps as the neighbors dispersed.

"Oh, Alice, I'm mortified!" she said. "I should have just thrown it out. I'd got it all sweaty running around the gym but it's kinda fun to wear, and . . ." She rested her arms across her knees and her head on her arms. "I'll never be able to face Lester again."

"Why? He knows you have *breasts*, Elizabeth!"

"It was a push-up bra, Alice, for girls who *don't*."

"But Les doesn't know that."

"Les knows everything about women," said Liz. "He can tell a push-up bra at twenty paces,

I'll bet." She tipped back her head and wailed, "Why does this have to happen to *me*?"

"Embarrassing stuff happens to all of us," I told her.

"Not like this! Not with a fire department announcing it to every neighbor on the block." And then she said, "I can remember every year of my life by something utterly humiliating that happened to me. Eleventh grade, the flammable bra; tenth grade, buying the Trojans; ninth grade. . . ."

"Liz, lighten up," I said. "*Nobody's* going to remember this except you. And Nathan, maybe, because of the fire trucks."

"Lester will."

"He won't. He's probably forgotten it already. He's got his mind on school and his thesis and graduation and—"

The screen door slammed behind us, and Lester came out on the porch.

"Gotta take off, Al," he said. "Take care." And as he went on down the sidewalk, he said over his shoulder, "Hey, Liz, the next time you decide to burn your bra, do it for a cause, huh?"

And then he was gone.

13

Out on the Town

On Monday a special assembly was called at school for twelve forty-five. All students were to attend, and names would be checked off at the doors to the auditorium.

"Well, I'll miss the first half of English lit, but it takes fifteen minutes off our lunch period," said Liz. "It's raining out, though, so we can't do much anyway. Save me a seat in the cafeteria."

We hate it when anything intrudes on our lunch period or when we all have to eat inside. I was halfway down the hall to geometry when I heard Amy Sheldon call my name. She used to be in special ed, but this year she's attending regular classes. I don't know quite what it is about Amy that rubs people the wrong way. She's small for her age, and her features are a bit out of alignment, but she looks essentially like everyone else. I guess it's her social awkwardness that makes her the butt of jokes. "Amy Clueless," some of the kids call her.

I had to rescue her at the Snow Ball last winter when she came to the dance alone and some girls were trying to humiliate her. She makes a good target, evidently, because you're never quite sure whether it affects her or not—if she even knows it's a joke. I've asked her before not to call out my name in the halls like she does, but it hasn't stopped her.

"Alice! Alice! Guess what?" she was yelling.

Kids started laughing and turning around, rolling their eyes. *Should I just keep going?* I wondered. *Duck into a classroom to shut her up?* I stopped and turned, frowning.

But she came on like a spinning top.

"Guess what?" she cried again. "I got my period yesterday! I really did!"

There were loud guffaws all around me, kids slowing down to listen in.

"Hey, Amy!" one girl called, fishing in her bag. "Want a tampon?"

"Yeah, Amy. Want a pad?" called another, and boys laughed.

Before I could get to her, Amy answered back, "I can't wear tampons yet, 'cause I'm a virgin, but I always carry them in case somebody else needs them."

The hall erupted in loud laughter, and Amy's comment was passed along from one group to another. You could hear laughter coming down the corridor, wave after wave, like dominoes falling.

I took her arm and hustled her on down the hall away from the catcalls. "Amy, that's something you don't talk about so everyone can hear," I said. "You don't want people laughing at you like that."

She looked at me blankly. "What's funny? I'm *glad* I got my period. I've been waiting and waiting!"

"I know, but it's bathroom stuff, so you just talk about it softly to other girls. Okay?"

"Okay. Mom says I'm a woman now and I have to be careful," she told me with satisfaction.

"She's right. You can never be too careful, Amy," I said. *Especially you,* I thought sadly, and gave her a little congratulatory pat on the back as I let her go.

"What do you suppose the assembly's about?" asked Liz as we found seats in the auditorium. "Some kind of compulsory sex ed, I'll bet."

"Nope. I'm guessing it's about discipline," said Gwen. "Whenever all students have to attend, you know it's discipline. A new set of rules."

Jill and Justin were sitting in front of us, and they thought so too.

"If we leave a book in our car, we'll probably need a pass to go back out and get it," said Justin.

Karen, sitting next to Jill, said, "Clothes. The principal will probably explain why we can't wear thongs."

"Who says we can't?" Gwen joked, and we laughed.

"See-through backpacks," said Sam, behind us.

But my thought was that the school was about to take away the open lunch period and make us stay on school property. Why else would they be taking up part of our lunch period for this?

Finally the principal came onstage. The *principal,* not the vice principal, so I figured it must be serious. Gradually the chatter died down, and when he said, "Good afternoon, students," everyone clammed up to see what the new restriction would be.

I was looking around for Pamela, because we always sit together at assemblies, but I couldn't see her, so I just assumed she was with Tim.

"Thank you all for attending," the principal continued, "especially those of you who are missing part of your lunch period. But we have two items of interest on the program. As you know, the faculty chooses one of our top seniors to be valedictorian at graduation. That has not been announced yet, but we have decided to honor three of our top students from each grade and to do this each year in a spring assembly. When I read the names, we would like the following students to come up onstage."

Well, *this* was a surprise. I think we were all relieved, and certainly curious. The principal read off three names from the freshman class, and there were cheers and applause after each one, as surprised students, somewhere in the auditorium, got awkwardly to their feet and made their way past the legs in their rows to get to the aisle.

The sophomore list.

Then the juniors. We whooped and cheered when Gwen was named, and we gave her backside slaps all the way down the row as she squeezed past us.

But what about Patrick? I wondered. Everyone knows he's a brain. And then I heard the principal announcing his name as one of the seniors. That's right. Patrick was a senior now. He was sitting down in the first row—something Patrick doesn't usually do, and I wondered if he'd gotten advance notice.

When all twelve students had been recognized, the principal gave their grade point averages and mentioned some of the activities they'd been involved in. Then he gave each of them a gold pin and a handshake, and when Gwen came back to sit with us, we passed the pin along so that we could all admire it and congratulate her again.

"And now," the principal said, "for the second part of this program we have a special treat. For the next two weekends, as you know, our music and drama departments will be giving performances of a great musical, *Guys and Dolls* . . ."

What? I thought. This assembly was going to be *fun*?

". . . And we're hoping that all of you will attend and bring your friends and families. To give you a taste of the music, we've asked the understudies of the four major parts to sing a few songs for you . . ."

Cheers and clapping. The understudies? That means Pamela!

". . . So may I present, *Guys and Dolls*!"

There was a drumroll, and I realized that Patrick and the other orchestra members had taken their places just below the stage. Mr. Kleingold, the conductor, brought down his baton, and the music began.

The guy who was playing the gambler, Sky Masterson, came out first in his slick suit and shoes, and he sang "Luck Be a Lady." He didn't have quite the voice of the guy who had been chosen number one for the part, but he'd do in a pinch, and he got a hearty round of applause. The understudy for Sister Sarah Brown came next and sang "If I Were a Bell." Then the crap game operator, Nathan Detroit, sang "Sue Me."

But it was Pamela who got the cheers when she came out from behind the curtain in a chorus girl's cat costume, complete with whiskers, ears, and a tail, and sang "Pet Me, Poppa" in her Brooklyn accent.

Guys stomped their feet and whistled, and just before she left the stage, she flirtatiously twirled her tail at the audience.

The principal said he'd see us all at the musical. The assembly was over, and Gwen and Liz and I rushed backstage to tell Pamela just how great she was. But Tim had got there first and was hugging a happy, glowing Pamela.

"You were fabulous!" we told her, and I think she actually began to believe us.

I did have a lot of fun with my feature on teachers' secrets, except that I changed the title to "Would You Ever Guess That . . . ?"

The first line was: *Would you ever guess that journalism teacher Shirley Ames once ate eleven and a half hot dogs to win a contest?*

I'd spent the whole week going to classes early to ask teachers for contributions, stayed late, stopped teachers in the hallways, interviewed them in the faculty lounge. . . . Some said they'd think it over and get back to me but never did. Others called me at home after I'd given them my number.

Would you ever guess that . . .
Bud Tolliver plays the ukulele?
Linda Jackson can belly dance?
Corina Galt owns a Model T?
Ernie Shepherd survived an avalanche?
Myra Bork raises ferrets?

"Kids are going to love this," Miss Ames said. "They'll never think of us in quite the same way. Every time they look at me, they'll think, 'Mustard and ketchup.'"

"Except there's so much more to each teacher than this," I said. "Next year maybe we could feature different teachers each month—every other issue—and tell about their backgrounds, families, hobbies. . . ."

"Yeah. I want to know how that sexy French

teacher spends her Saturday nights," said Tony.

"Let's put that feature—no, not the French teacher—on the agenda for next year, Alice," Miss Ames said. "You'll have to help us remember, though, because all our seniors will be gone."

"Just my luck," said Tony.

The last week of rehearsals was wild. School in the morning, rehearsals each afternoon till eight or nine at night, stuff to write for the newspaper, leftovers to eat when I got home, then homework till midnight or later, and I was up again at six.

"You're trying to do too much," Dad told me one morning when I appeared zombielike at breakfast and knocked over my orange juice.

To tell the truth, I had one of the better jobs on stage crew. The art department had pitched in on most of the sets, and we'd rented a couple backdrops for select scenes, so all I had left to do was a little more painting: a lamppost here, a few bricks there, a table—things like that—extending a set or filling one in.

I didn't have to be one of Molly's prop girls who dashed onstage between scenes and moved stuff around, and being careful not to leave out something important, something a character needed in one of the scenes.

But I was supposed to help out as needed, so I

made myself Pamela's personal costume changer between scenes. I had copies of Adelaide's costumes at the ready in case the original Adelaide broke an arm or something and Pamela had to go on. A lot of the time, though, I sat far back in the auditorium and did homework during rehearsals, waiting to see if I was needed.

I was actually glad not to be spending more time with Patrick right then, seeing what Pamela was going through. Tim hung around some of the rehearsals, and the minute Mr. Kleingold or Mr. Ellis called it quits for the night, he would whisk Pamela away and drive her home. Or they'd go somewhere to eat.

If I'd still been going out with Sam Mayer, for instance, his hovering would have driven me over the edge. It's nice to get a back rub when you're tired or a kiss when you're discouraged, but sometimes you just need time to get stuff done, and the less demands on you, the better.

Everyone on stage crew was allowed to take off one of the six performances to watch the show from the audience, as long as he had someone cover for him. One of the prop girls said she'd look after Pamela's costumes for me, so I decided to attend the musical on the first Saturday night, which would be the third performance. I wanted to sit with Liz and Gwen, and that was the night Molly was going to be included in the curtain call; she had chemo again the following week, so she wanted to attend when she felt her best.

Dad had let us put up one of the *Guys and Dolls* posters in the window of the Melody Inn, and I mentioned it to every customer who came in that day.

David, I noticed, was unusually quiet and seemed absorbed in some order sheets that Dad had asked him to tally. Except that when I stopped by the office on my ten-minute break, he didn't seem to be looking at the papers in front of him at all—he was just sliding his thumbnail up and down the edge of the account book.

I knew then.

"David?" I said. "You ended it with Connie, didn't you?"

He slowly raised his head and looked in my direction. "Yes," he said.

"Is that what you're thinking about? Whether you did the right thing?"

He smiled and shook his head. "No. I'm at peace with that. I'm just wondering if I did it the right way, and I'm sorry she's taking it so hard. And sorry that when we broke up the first time, I didn't make it stick, so she wouldn't have to go through it again. But this time I'm sure."

I waited. How do you know what to ask? How do you know when to just listen? Your gut feeling, that's all. But I let my curiosity get the better of me. "Did you go camping together? Is that when you told her?"

"You guessed it," he said.

"Only because you told me you probably would. Go camping, I mean." And I thought about David and his girlfriend sitting out under the stars on a romantic night and then David telling her it was over.

"You told her *that night*, or the next morning?"

"Actually, we talked all night long," he said.

"I don't understand love," I said after a moment.

"Neither do I. Human love, anyway," said David. "But I understand love of God, and that's why I'm at peace."

"I don't think I'd ever be able to make that choice."

"You don't have to. Not everyone is called to be a priest or a nun, and you're not even Catholic."

"But if the pope changes his mind and says it's okay for priests to marry, won't you be mad?"

"No, because if Connie was the right girl for me, maybe I would have decided differently," he said.

This wasn't making any sense, because how did David know that he just hadn't found the right girl yet, that she wasn't still out there somewhere, just waiting to be discovered?

"Listen, David," I said suddenly. "Does the fact that you're going into the priesthood mean that you can't have any fun?"

"Of course not!"

"Then what are you doing tonight?" I asked.

"What?"

"Tonight. Do you have any plans?"

"I hadn't thought much about it, actually."

"Then how about going to see *Guys and Dolls* with me and my friends? We'll pick you up around seven, and I'll even pay for your ticket."

He looked surprised. "Well, hey! How can I refuse? That had a long run on Broadway, didn't it?"

"Yes, and it'll be a blast tonight because one of our friends is in it. Where do you live?"

"In the District. I think I'll stay here at the store, though, and put in some overtime. Pick me up at seven. I'll be ready," he said.

14

The Diner with David

"You did *what*?" asked Liz.

"I invited a priest to go with us tonight. Well, a priest-to-be, and we're picking him up at seven," I said. "He's cool. I already told Gwen. She'll get him after she picks up Molly."

"This is wild!" Liz said. "You're not trying to tempt him, are you?"

"No, Liz. I'm saving him from another night of beer with the boys, that's all."

Liz and I were on the porch when Gwen pulled up, and David slid over in the backseat to make room. He was wearing jeans, cowboy boots, a black turtleneck, and a jean jacket.

"Hi, Molly! Hi, Gwen!" I said. "Liz, this is David, and tonight he's our guest for . . . Yay! The high school musical!"

"Bet it's been a while since you've seen one of those," said Liz.

"*Seen* one? I've *been* in one, and not so long ago, either," David told us. "You may not believe this, but I was the Royal Canadian Mountie in *Rose Marie*."

"What's that?" asked Molly.

"A musical so old that nobody does it anymore. We did it in a sort of camp style. The year before we had done *Hair*, and several of our more conservative citizens were upset, so we did the revival of *Rose Marie* to placate them."

"And you sang?" asked Gwen.

"Did I *sing*? You bet'cha. In full uniform. I was even in *The Mikado* in community theater."

"The Secret Life of David Reilly," I said, and we were on our way to the school.

Molly refused to wear a wig. She had on her trademark baseball cap, but she chose one with sparkles and spangles for this night. She'd even glued some sparkles on her sneakers. She had no eyebrows or eyelashes—those fall out too temporarily from chemo—but she wore makeup and had glitter on her cheeks that made her eyes dance.

"I want a good look at those lampposts—see if they got them right," she said. "And the low curtain in the Save-a-Soul Mission. I told them it's got to look faded. I found a storefront church in D.C. that said we could use theirs."

At the school Molly went backstage to sit with the crew while Gwen and Liz and David and I found ninth-row seats. The full orchestra was in place, and the auditorium was packed. The assembly had been good advertising for it. David seemed as eager for the curtain to rise as we did.

The overture began. I didn't have a good view of the orchestra pit, but my ears were tuned to percussion—I'm better at that than the melody—and I knew that Patrick was there. Finally the curtain went up, and the scene was New York City, with actors and actresses parading around Times Square. Pamela, as a member of the chorus, looked great.

There were no big mishaps that I could see—the girl who played Adelaide didn't break a leg or anything that would have given Pamela the role—and the enthusiasm of the audience made the singers perform even better. At the curtain call, after the whole cast had taken their bows, Mr. Ellis called the crew onstage, and I felt tears in my eyes when Molly was introduced as the prop manager. When she stepped out from behind the curtain, I grabbed David's hands and made him clap extra loud. Everyone stood and gave her a standing ovation.

Pamela was going out with Tim after the show, and we didn't want to keep Molly up too late, so as soon as we could collect her from backstage, we got in the car. David said, "Molly, when's curfew for you?"

"No curfew," she said, "but I fold around eleven."

"Then how about some food? My favorite place, and it's on me," David told us.

"Great!" said Gwen. "Just give me the directions."

Twenty minutes later, after many twists and turns, we pulled up in front of the Tastee Diner in Bethesda and piled out.

It was one of the old original diners, modeled after a dining car on a train. A backboard of shiny fan-shaped aluminum stood behind the stacks of plates and saucers, and the short-order cook expertly tended to fried eggs, burgers, sausages, and fries, all cooking at once on the grill.

"Hi, David!" the grill man said. "How's it goin'?" Then he looked at us and said, with a wink, "Pretty good, huh?"

"David!" called the waitress who was holding the coffeepot and filling a customer's cup. "Nice to see ya!"

"You must come here pretty often, huh?" I asked as we took a corner booth, all five of us squeezing in.

"As often as I can," David said. "Some friends introduced me to the Tastee Diner last year, and I'll take any excuse I can get to come out here."

It was popular with everyone else as well. Teen couples on first dates, apparently—a little too polite and self-conscious; gangs of girls in hooded sweatshirts, with private school logos on the front; guys and girls back from a game; a homeless man or two with matted hair and just enough money for some coffee and bacon; an off-duty bus driver ordering the turkey dinner, with extra gravy; and a small seventy-ish woman eating chipped beef on toast.

We eyed the menu and the coconut layer cake there on a pedestal beside the cash register. The middle-aged waitress was smiling as she came over. "Well, I knew you must have a love life, David, but I never suspected *four* girlfriends," she joked. "Coffee's on us tonight. Where y'all been?"

We told her about the musical.

"Oh, I loved that show!" she said. "And who would have thought that Marlon Brando could sing?"

Gwen was checking out the menu, and I could tell by the funny rise of an eyebrow that everything on it was a caloric disaster. *Pork chops and gravy, ribs and fries, macaroni and cheese, fried chicken and biscuits. . . .* "David, how do you stay so thin?" she asked. "Wow, but it looks good."

We settled for a club sandwich, two burgers, a couple of chocolate malteds, and a short stack for David. When the food arrived, miraculously fast considering that the waitress gave the order in code, it was exactly right.

During a lull, the cook came over to chat. "What's the occasion?" he asked David. "Night on the town?"

"Went to see *Guys and Dolls* at their high school," David answered. "Lots of fun."

"What's it about? Gangstas?"

"Deceit, deception, redemption . . ."

"And the Salvation Army," Molly added.

"Huh," said the cook, puzzled. "No accounting for taste."

When the cook went back to his grill and we were savoring our malteds, I noticed how skillfully David kept the conversation on the present. He seemed to be taking his cues from Molly. If she talked about what courses she was going to take next year, then he talked about next year. If she focused on school productions in the past, David went with that. He was usually future oriented, and if Molly hadn't been with us, he would probably have asked about Liz's plans for college, what Gwen hoped to become. He had the ability to look straight into your eyes when he talked to you, as though you were the most important person in the world.

He'll make a good priest, I thought. At the same time, *He'd make a good husband and father.*

We watched the parade of night owls come in—an old man wanting a plate of bacon and toast; father and son for cheeseburgers; a slightly drunk woman for coffee; three college girls back from a movie.

"A microcosm of humanity," said David.

Molly smiled with satisfaction and took one last swallow of her malted. "Whatever," she said. "It's been a fun evening."

When I got home at last around midnight, Dad and Sylvia had gone to bed. I'd turned my cell phone off during the performance, so I checked it just before I went to sleep. Only one call. From Patrick. No message.

I slept until noon the next day. Dad and Sylvia were at church. I toasted an English muffin, buttered it, set the saucer on the floor when I was through so that Annabelle could lick the remaining butter. Then I read the comics and finally picked up *Heart of Darkness* to finish before class on Monday.

By mid-afternoon, when Patrick still hadn't called, I punched in his number.

"Hi," I said when he answered. "What's up?"

"Oh," said Patrick. "Hi. What'd you think of the performance? Not that you haven't watched it a dozen times."

"Not from out front, though—not all the way through," I said. "I thought it went pretty well. Pamela looked so natural up there, I think she was born for the stage."

"You didn't see me wave at you?" Patrick asked.

I paused. "When? From the orchestra pit? No, I guess not. It was sort of dark in there."

"Oh," said Patrick. "Thought you saw me."

"I didn't see you wave," I said.

"My mistake."

Where was this conversation going? I wondered.

"I guess I thought you'd be hanging out after—with Pamela and everything," Patrick went on.

"No. She went out with Tim. We'd brought Molly."

"Well, I'd thought maybe we could go somewhere after, but I guess you had other plans."

"Sorry, Patrick! I didn't know you wanted to! I'm not a mind reader."

"Yeah. Well, we were both at the same place at the same time. . . ."

Are guys especially programmed to drive you nuts or what? "Patrick, we're both at the same place at the same time when we're at school, and we don't wait for each other after," I said.

"Good point. So . . . where *did* you go?" he asked.

"We had a full car. Gwen was driving."

"Yeah?"

"I was so glad Molly could go up onstage. And everyone gave her a standing ovation. I almost cried."

"Yeah, I gave her a little drumroll. Did you notice? You didn't tell me where you went after, though."

"We went to the Tastee Diner."

"And who was the guy?"

The guy? Aha! So this was it! "David?" I said, innocently.

"You're asking me? I don't know. Was that his name?"

"Yes! David! He works part-time at the Melody Inn."

"And the rest of the time?"

"A student at Georgetown."

"Really? I didn't know you knew anyone at Georgetown," said Patrick.

"Only because he works for Dad." I hoped Patrick couldn't hear the smile in my voice.

"So . . . he's a college man, right?"

Oh wow! Was Patrick ever jealous!

"Yes, he's a college man." I couldn't help myself from adding, "He just broke up with his girlfriend, Patrick, and I was trying to cheer him up."

There was silence. "And . . . *did* you cheer him up? When I looked, you had your hands all over him."

I remembered that I'd had grabbed David's hands and made him clap extra hard for Molly. "We *all* cheered him up, Patrick. Gwen and Liz and Molly and I. We had a good time and so did he." Then I decided to take pity on him. "Patrick, do you know *why* he broke up with his girlfriend?"

"Do I want to know this?"

"Yes. He's going to become a priest."

"Oh!" said Patrick.

"I don't understand you," I said, still hoping he wouldn't detect the smile in my voice. "You didn't seem to care when I went to the dance with Scott."

"Scott I can understand," said Patrick. "But College Man . . ."

"You're going to be a college guy yourself pretty soon."

"Then maybe you'll invite *me* out with your girlfriends?" said Patrick, and we laughed.

We talked a little more about school, about homework, about Patrick's dad retiring from the foreign service, and finally he said he had to study for a test and we said good-bye.

I turned off my cell phone. Then I stood up and looked at myself in the mirror. I looked pretty good. I was grinning.

He's jealous! He's jealous! I said to myself as I danced around and around the room. I never thought it would happen.

The following week everyone connected to the show was a zombie. We were trying to catch up on all the assignments we had missed the week before, and we still had three more performances to get through the coming weekend, with more rehearsals every day after school. Some teachers were understanding about it, some weren't. But finally it was the weekend, and I was able to give Pamela my full attention backstage.

Adelaide's chorus girls had to change costumes the most, and Pamela was afraid she'd get her period and leak through her satin pants. But every show went off without a hitch, and on the final night, as I watched Pamela onstage, I felt a little down. Envious again. Jealous, even, and it bothered me. She'd dash backstage with the other chorus girls, and all I had to do was have her costume ready. Help yank off the pink top and pull on the blue. Unzip the satin shorts and help her step into a skirt. Zip her up, put on the headpiece, give her an encouraging pat, and send her off again.

What was I, anyway? A mother hen? I got to write a feature story about the musical, of course, but was that it? Was I just a byline? A shoulder to lean on? Was it so much to ask that just once in my life, I'd get to walk onstage in front of a zillion people in an auditorium with crystal chandeliers and receive a prestigious award to the wild applause of admirers?

Well, okay. Without the chandeliers, maybe.

And maybe not a *zillion* people.

And maybe not *wild* applause.

But when would *I* get a little public appreciation and recognition, just for me? For something important? When would I get to say, *Thank you very much*?

Not this night, evidently, because Pamela rushed back to tell me I had handed her the wrong shoes, and she barely made it onstage in time.

• • •

What I really did feel bad about was that Pamela didn't invite her mom to the show. Didn't even tell her she was in it. Her dad came, bringing Meredith, and they came backstage with a little bouquet from the grocery store, like many of the other parents did. But I couldn't understand why Mrs. Jones couldn't have come to a performance. She would have loved it, loved seeing Pamela up there.

"Why *didn't* you invite her, Pamela?" I'd asked.

"Are you kidding?" she'd answered. "She would have embarrassed me! She'd be trying to outdo all the other moms by cheering and carrying on. She's breaking her neck trying to be 'The Good Mom,' and the harder she tries, the more it turns me off."

Pamela brought Tim to the cast party on the second Saturday night, of course, and I could tell he was relieved that the musical was finally over and he'd have Pamela to himself. I'd missed the cast party last year because I was sick, but this time I rode over with Patrick. Orchestra members hadn't been invited, but cast and crew were allowed to bring dates.

The guy who played Sky Masterson was having the party at his house—a big house in

Kensington—and his folks even had caterers in the kitchen, serving up Coney Island hot dogs and Junior's cheesecake from New York. Patrick was wearing a black shirt with his jeans, and stage crew wore black too, so we wouldn't be so visible in the wings.

At the party the main characters got to perform all over again. They put on little skits—dance routines and parodies of songs that they'd obviously cooked up in advance for the party. The senior who played Adelaide, Kelsey Reeves, did a really funny takeoff of a stripper, except that just when you thought she was down to bare skin—and I could tell that Mr. Ellis was looking nervous—we saw that she was wearing a body stocking with signatures of the entire cast written all over it.

Pamela, as her understudy, did a tap dance with a top hat twirling on one finger, and Sky Masterson and Sarah Brown sang a duet.

The funniest act, though, was the one the three directors—Mr. Ellis, Mr. Gage, and Miss Ortega—put on. The two men played guitars, and Miss Ortega wore a long silky tunic and a blond wig with bangs. They pretended to be the folksinger trio Peter, Paul, and Mary, popular back in the sixties. They sang "Puff, the Magic Dragon" but completely overacted, which made us howl with laughter.

Mostly we stage crew members just watched and applauded, and I thought to myself, *Well, if it weren't for the audience, there wouldn't be anyone to perform* for, *would there?* Besides, I was content just to be there with Patrick, even though he had a headache from three nights of staying up late and playing the drums. We kissed in the car when he took me home, but I know it's not easy to be romantic when you have a headache—or a cold, a sore throat, cramps. So I told him to go home and get some sleep, and he seemed grateful.

But I was feeling dissatisfied, not with Patrick, but with myself. Looking over the past few months, I couldn't help thinking that Liz got to chase a cute guy around the school gym to a cheering crowd; Pamela got to tap dance; Gwen got an award in front of the whole school; but the only applause I'd received so far was for climbing out of a coffin, and I'd almost missed my cue to do *that*. I *had* to be good at *some*thing, but it was taking me a long time to find out what.

15

Waiting

There was only one more full month left of school,
and it made us crazy. Seniors could more or less
coast—they had their colleges nailed down, their
jobs for the summer; that was my theory, anyway. I guess we always think that seniors have it
made.

My SAT results had come back, and they
were better than my PSAT scores—not fabulous,
but pretty darn respectable, and I decided I'd let
them stand. It tired me out to keep comparing
them against everyone else's scores, especially
Gwen's or Patrick's. I kept thinking about the
way I compare myself to others, to my friends.
Why I couldn't seem to be content to just be *me*.
On the whole, it had been a pretty good year,
and I thought of all the people for whom it had
been bad. Molly, for example. Brian Brewster, for
another, though I wasn't sorry for him in the least.

Amy Sheldon, for whom every year, it seemed, was a bad year.

I was thinking about what I might propose for *The Edge* when I went to our planning session on Wednesday. My feature story on the Day of Silence had been well received, though it hadn't made the huge buzz I'd hoped for. Hadn't stirred up much controversy, and perhaps that was good. It would be great if we didn't even *need* a Day of Silence to remind us what gays go through. Didn't need a GSA. But still, it would have been nice to get a *little* more attention.

A lot of kids liked the article about teachers' secrets, and everyone liked the photos of *Guys and Dolls,* thanks to our photographers, Don and Sam.

"What do we have for our last two issues?" Miss Ames asked.

"We already decided to delay the final issue until we get some pics of the prom," Scott said. "And we always do a farewell piece for any teacher who's leaving."

He went around the table, asking each of us in turn what we had for the next issue. "What about features, Alice?" he asked.

I read off the list of ideas I'd been keeping in a notebook: a story on favorite hangouts, an article on the school parking lot situation, the current policy on suspensions and expulsions, summer footwear with photos, student representation at school board meetings. . . .

"All good," said Scott. "Let's see what you work up first."

After the meeting I was all the way down to my locker before I realized I'd left my jacket in Room 17. I turned around and went back, and just as I reached the journalism classroom, I heard Don say, "We're good for Saturday night, then—you and Kendra and Christy and me?"

"Yeah, we're on," Scott answered.

Then Don: "You and Kendra are really tight, huh?"

And Scott: "I guess so. She's even talking about switching colleges and coming to mine."

"No kidding?"

I took three steps backward as they came out the door and bent quickly over the drinking fountain as they started down the hall. Rising up, I swallowed the gulp of water and said, "Forgot my jacket. See ya!"

"See ya," said Scott.

"Take care," said Don.

I went inside the empty classroom and slowly put on my jacket. I guess a lot had happened in the last two months since the Sadie Hawkins Day dance. Maybe Scott had agreed to go with me because he wasn't sure of Kendra. Maybe Kendra hadn't been sure of him. And maybe I had invited Scott because I wasn't sure of my feelings for Patrick.

In any case, the crush was definitely over, and I was almost relieved to hear that Scott and Kendra were "together," and he was out of my dreams for good.

The first week of May was spent on catch-up. Catching up on all the homework I'd let slide, the papers that were late, the feature story I was writing for *The Edge,* straightening my messy room, doing my wash, answering e-mails. . . .

I took time out to give Sylvia a hand in the garden after work on Saturday, though—the first Saturday of May—and it helped chill me out. The lawn had been so torn up during the renovation that we had all new shrubs planted along one side, and Sylvia splurged on tulips and daffodils, already in bloom when we replanted them: purples and yellows in one place, reds and yellows in another.

"If you hadn't become a teacher, would you be a gardener?" I asked, seeing how much pleasure she took in it.

She chuckled. "Gardening's one of the things I enjoy part-time, but I'm not sure I'd want to make it my life's work."

"Did you ever want to be anything else? Like a . . . Shakespearian actress or something?"

"I don't know that the stage can support too many Shakespearian actresses, Alice, though it might be fun to work at it for a summer. No, I think I'd miss the interaction with students. An audience doesn't give that much feedback. And I'd probably be bored with so much attention to myself," she said.

That was a strange thought, I decided. I didn't think performers ever got tired of themselves. But maybe they had to be constantly fed by an audience in order to feel good about it. Still, could you really get tired of a life of applause and adulation?

"Where should we put these?" I asked, lifting up the last pot of white tulips—SNOW WHITES, the little tag read.

Sylvia thought for a minute. "You know, I think they deserve a spot all to themselves. They're not as showy as the reds, but they're beautiful in another way. Let's give them a green backdrop—right over here—and let them have center stage."

Dad and Sylvia were going out that night, and I was tired from all the gardening. I didn't really want to go anywhere, but I didn't want to spend the evening alone, either. I called Liz.

"You doing anything tonight?" I asked. Liz has gone out with a guy three times since the Sadie Hawkins Day dance—not the same guy, either—and probably had a waiting list, but I asked anyway.

"A guy in my biology class said he'd call, but a girl told me he's a 'hands-on' type of guy, so I was going to make some excuse if he did," she said.

Every time Liz has a date, I want to call out the cheering section, but then I remember what Patrick said about how a lot of reassurance can make somebody insecure. So I just played it cool, like, *Of course guys like you! Why would they not?*

"Want to sleep over, then?" I said. "Eight o'clock? Earlier, if you want. I imagine Pamela's out with Tim, but I'll call anyway. Gwen, I know, is at her aunt's for the weekend."

I called Pamela on her cell phone, and it was a while before she answered.

"Hello?" she said finally.

"How you doing? I thought maybe you were out with Tim," I said. "Liz is going to sleep over."

"He's got a really bad cold," Pamela told me. "I suppose I'll catch it next."

"Then you want to come? Dad and Sylvia are out."

There was an uncharacteristic pause. "Yeah," she said finally. "I guess so."

"Don't let me twist your arm."

"No, I'll come," she said. "Will Gwen be there?"

"She's at her aunt's. Come about eight, okay?"

"See you," she said.

The usual letdown after a performance, I thought. The stage crew feels it, but it's worse for the cast. All that attention, the footlights, the spotlight, the costumes, the makeup . . . For six weeks or so, you're part of a group, a family, a team, a production. You're all involved in the same thing—the excitement, the inside jokes, the sharing—and then . . . poof! It's over. *Fini.* I checked the freezer for Pamela's favorite ice cream, coffee. *Perfecto.*

Liz arrived first and brought some brownies she'd made. "Everything cleaned up at your place?" I asked her, realizing I hadn't seen cleaning crews outside her house for a while.

"We were able to wash down some of the walls, but the hall had to be repainted," she said. "And of course we had to replace the dryer. Dad's getting over it now, but he was so mad at me! I don't think he'll be buying me a car anytime soon."

Pamela didn't realize she'd forgotten her

sleeping bag until she walked in. "I'll go back," she said.

"Never mind," I said. "You can sleep on the couch. Come on. Liz brought brownies."

I brought out the whole half gallon of ice cream, and we carried our bowls into the family room, making brownie sundaes. Pamela settled down with a little sigh and spooned ice cream into her mouth.

"Post-performance letdown?" I said.

"I guess. Everything happens at once."

"I know what you mean. How's Tim?"

"He sounded awful on the phone. Temperature, too. He says he's probably contagious, so he's staying in this weekend."

"Lucky for us!" said Liz. "Girlfriend time! I wish Gwen were here, but she's got so much family, somebody's always celebrating something."

"That must be nice," I said. "I've got to go all the way to Chicago or Tennessee to see my relatives."

We rehashed old news, new news, tidbits, gossip. . . .

"You heard about Jill and Justin, didn't you?" asked Liz.

"They didn't break up, did they?" I asked.

"Are you kidding? They're plastered together with industrial-strength glue!"

"Yeah, I heard that Justin's parents took them both to the Bahamas over spring break," said Pamela. "First they were going to take Justin alone to get him away from her; then they ended up taking them both."

"Well, that's not quite the way it happened," Liz confided. "I got it straight from Karen. Mr. and Mrs. Collier took Justin to the Bahamas, all right, to get him away from Jill, whom they consider to be a grade-A gold digger. But guess who showed up at the hotel next door? Justin sent her the money, and Jill flew in. His folks were furious."

"Omigod!" I said. "Why didn't we hear about this before?"

"We don't move in the same circles, I guess. I don't have any classes with them, do you?" said Liz.

"No. I think his parents better give in," I said. "It's a losing battle. They've been together a long time."

"Karen says the Colliers are hoping that college will put a brake on the romance. Get them as far away from each other as possible."

"Unless she follows him there," I said, thinking about Scott and Kendra.

"And she probably will," said Liz.

We all sat pondering that a minute.

Then Pamela said, "I'm two weeks late."

I had just reached for a pillow. Then I paused. Looked at Pamela. "What?"

Pamela's voice was softer now. "My period's two weeks late."

I think I stopped breathing. Elizabeth was staring.

"You think . . . you're *pregnant*?" Liz asked.

"I . . . I don't know." Pamela swallowed.

I let go of the pillow and leaned back, studying her face. "But . . . but you said you were using condoms!" My heart was pounding.

"We were. Well, most of the time."

I didn't want to hear this. "Most of the time?"

"Well, except for a couple of times during rehearsals. I'd hardly had any time for Tim, and he was feeling left out. . . . But it was still five days from the middle of my period!"

"Five days!" I exclaimed. "But, Pamela, sometimes your period isn't regular!"

She sucked in her breath and it sounded shaky. "Don't make me feel worse," she pleaded.

I wanted to grab her and shake her. I wanted to hug her. I wasn't sure what I wanted to do.

"Maybe it's just all the tension and everything from the musical," Liz said quickly. "You *have* been under a lot of stress, Pamela. And all that strenuous dancing. My periods are off sometimes when I'm upset."

"That's what I keep telling myself," Pamela said. "But . . . two weeks?"

I couldn't take my eyes off her. She seemed so tiny all of a sudden, like a little girl. How could a little girl be having a little baby? It was as though we were back in sixth grade when I'd first met Pamela Jones, and she had blond hair so long she could sit on it. She could sing and dance and got to play Rosebud, the leading role, in the class play. All I got to be was a "bramble bush with branches thick," and I was so jealous. I sure wasn't jealous now.

"Have you said anything to Tim?" I asked.

"Not yet. He's miserable enough with that cold. I don't want to worry him about this."

"You're right," I said. "You could start getting it at any time, and it would be all this worry for nothing." But even I didn't believe it.

"If . . . what if I *am* . . . ?" She stopped as though she couldn't even say the word. Her voice was even softer than before.

"Well, it won't change anything between you and me and Liz, you know that. Gwen, either."

"Don't tell Gwen," said Pamela.

"Why not?" I asked. "We're not telling anybody, but if we did, why not Gwen?"

"Just because." Pamela fidgeted with a hole in the knee of her jeans. "She's so smart and . . ."

220 • Almost Alice

"But she's had intercourse!" Elizabeth said. I always laugh when Liz says *intercourse* instead of *sex*. But it didn't seem funny now.

"I don't want Gwen to know because she's too smart to get pregnant," said Pamela.

"Stupidity and carelessness aren't necessarily the same," I told her. "But even if you *are* pregnant, and that's a big 'if,' Pamela, it's your story to tell, not ours."

"Thanks," said Pamela, and her voice was shaky again.

"Listen." I studied her for a moment. "Why don't you just buy a pregnancy test kit and . . ."

"No!" cried Pamela. "I'm not *ready* for that!"

"Let's watch a movie," said Liz.

We put in a DVD and moved to the couch, sitting side by side, Pamela between us. I don't know if any of us really watched or what. All I could think about was Pamela, and I felt sick to my stomach.

For the next week I felt as though I wanted to call Pamela every fifteen minutes to see if her period had started yet. I thought about her when I was supposed to be studying for an exam. I worried about her when I should have been writing a feature story.

I e-mailed her about trivial things so that if

she'd happened to have started her period and forgotten to tell me, she'd think of it then. Nothing.

At school Pamela went around with a drawn look on her face. She wasn't throwing up. She didn't say she was nauseated. She just looked thinner, was quieter at lunch, distracted when we went to Starbucks after school. Every once in a while she would laugh loudly at something somebody said, as though she were just tuning in occasionally and had to let us know. She even seemed more distant from Tim, I noticed, when they were together.

On Saturday she called.

"I told Tim last night," she said.

"Told him that . . . ?"

"That I'm over three weeks late. He wanted to have sex, and I just didn't feel like it, so I . . . I told him."

"What did he say, Pamela?"

"What *could* he say? All the right things, of course. That maybe it was just stress, but that if I *was* pregnant, he'd be here for me. But what does it really mean, Alice—'I'll be here for you'? For what, exactly? He can't have the baby for me, can he?"

"He's trying to be supportive, Pamela." I didn't even like to hear the word *baby*.

She was crying now. "I know. I could tell he

was upset. Shocked, even. Oh, he kissed me and told me not to worry, that he loved me no matter what, but . . . we're both scared. Why did this have to happen to *us*, Alice? Jill and Justin have been having sex forever, and *she's* not pregnant!"

"Don't you think it's time to take a pregnancy test? Do you know how soon it would tell?" I asked.

There was a tremulous little sigh at the other end of the line. "I'm too scared to find out."

"But if you're not pregnant, Pamela, you could stop all this worrying and waiting!"

"Will you come with me to buy one? You and Liz?" she asked.

"Of course," I said.

Ironic that we celebrated Mother's Day that Sunday. Next year, maybe, I'd be sending a *Happy Mother's Day to a Friend* card to Pamela, and I couldn't bear to think about it.

I'd already bought a gift for Sylvia, though, and when Dad said we were going to take her to a buffet brunch at the Crowne Plaza, I tucked it in my bag and climbed into the backseat with Les.

It's impossible to be serious and moody if Les isn't. First of all, Sylvia still wasn't "mom" to us, but here we were, celebrating Mother's Day. And second, it felt weird to be sitting in the backseat with Lester, like young kids on an outing with their parents.

And suddenly Lester whined, "Are we there yet?"

Sylvia's tinkling laughter filled the car, and I could see Dad's grin in the rearview mirror. But before either of them could respond, Les said, "Alice is making faces at me, Dad!"

I jumped in with, "He started it!"

"She's over on my side! Make her move, Dad!" Les continued.

"Huh-*uh*!" I croaked. "Here's the line, and you're way over where you're not supposed to be!"

"One more word out of either of you, and it's no dessert, and that's final," Dad said.

We were still laughing when we entered the restaurant.

I liked that we looked like a family, though. Liked that I was beginning to feel that Sylvia was family too. At the buffet table Sylvia asked for sour cream, then got distracted and walked on. When the server came back with the little container, he gave it to me and I liked that he said, "Would you give this to your mom?"

After the meal, when we were having coffee, I slipped a card across the table. "Happy Mama's Day," I said.

Sylvia gave me a surprised smile. "Well, *thank*

you, Alice!" she said, and opened it. Inside was a gift certificate for one pet grooming session at *Fur and Feathers* for Annabelle: hair trimmed, coat brushed, claws filed, teeth brushed, ears cleaned—the works.

If Sylvia remembered the bitter words I'd spoken last November about her cat—*our* cat—she didn't show it. She just gave me a full smile, and her eyes were warm and friendly. "This means a lot," she said. And it did.

16

Tears

On Monday, two days before my birthday, Pamela, Liz, and I went to the CVS store after school, moving woodenly down the aisle of sanitary products, condoms, lubricants, ointments, and finally—pregnancy test kits.

I didn't want to be doing this! We should be looking at college catalogs! Summer sandals! At sunscreen and sunglasses! We should be planning parties and raft trips and bike rides and picnics, not thinking about baby clothes in nine months. *Eight* months!

But it was hard not to think about babies. The end of each aisle had a little bouquet of spring flowers on it. The gift wrap featured baby chicks and bunnies. Advertising signs placed here and there were done up in yellow, pink, and blue.

When we found the test kits, Pamela said, "Keep an eye out at each end of the row, will you?

All I need is for someone from school to see me. Or for a neighbor to tell Dad."

I moved to one end of the aisle and stared at remedies for yeast infections. Liz moved to tampons at the other end.

It took longer than we thought, because Pamela wanted to read the directions for each test kit before she finally chose one. We covered for her at the cash register, too, to make sure no one we knew was around. But when we got outside and I asked Pamela where she wanted to take the test, she said, "I'm not going to do it yet, because maybe I just didn't ovulate this month, with all the tension. Maybe I've just skipped a period. I'll wait one more week, and then I'll do it."

"Any morning sickness or anything?" I asked.

"No, just a little queasy sometimes, but I think that's because I'm not sleeping very well."

Isn't that the same as nausea? I wondered, but I didn't push it. We left her at the corner of her street, then Liz and I walked slowly home.

I thought of all the times we'd taken this same walk, on this same sidewalk, with no other worries than whether or not you were supposed to close your eyes when you kissed. When the future stretched endlessly before us—high school, college, on and on. And now, for one of us, maybe, this huge detour. . . .

Finally Liz said, "If, like we promised, we don't tell anyone . . . and something happens to Pamela . . ."

"Don't even *think* it!" I said.

By Tuesday morning I thought *I* was going to be sick. Scenes kept running through my head: Pamela telling her dad and Meredith; Tim facing his folks; the accusations, the tears, the lectures, the anger. . . . It wasn't just Pamela and Tim's lives that would be disrupted, but their families' as well.

But maybe Pamela *wasn't* pregnant! Maybe she was . . . maybe she wasn't . . . maybe she was. . . .

"What's with you?" Gwen asked Pam at lunch when she didn't finish her turkey wrap. "You usually eat yours and bum a pickle off me too!"

Pamela faked a laugh. "Watching my weight," she said.

"Yeah. Right, skinny gal. You don't want that oatmeal cookie? I'll take it."

I changed the subject. "How's Molly? Anyone check on her lately?"

"Looking good, as far as I can tell," said Gwen. "Her mom said her blood tests definitely showed improvement. New combination of drugs, I guess."

"Well, at least something's going right for one of us," Pamela said as the bell rang, and I saw Gwen studying her closely.

After school Liz and I sat out on the new screened porch behind our family room. The azalea bushes were in bloom, the grass was thick and green, the first bumblebee of the season was buzzing slowly around outside the screen, and a light breeze blew through from the southeast, hypnotically caressing our faces.

"Do you think . . . if she *is* pregnant . . . she's eating okay?" Liz asked me. "Have you noticed if she drinks milk with lunch?"

I shook my head.

"I mean, is she supposed to be taking vitamins or anything?"

"You're asking *me*?" I said.

We were quiet some more.

"Is it possible she's already taken the test and just doesn't want to tell us?" I said aloud. And then, answering my own question, "With Pamela, anything's possible."

"Maybe we should set up a doctor's appointment and just take her there by force," Liz said.

"Yeah. Right."

"We could tell her there's someone we want her to meet."

"And then he tells her to climb up on the

table and put her feet in the stirrups?" I turned my head suddenly and listened. "Was that the doorbell?"

I got up and went back through the family room, the kitchen, the hallway, and opened the front door. There was Pamela, holding the test kit.

"Are you alone?" she asked as I pulled her inside.

"Liz is here, that's all," I told her.

"I guess . . . I'm ready," said Pamela.

I got Liz, and the three of us went upstairs. We sat together in my bedroom—Pamela and me on the bed, Liz on the desk chair.

"Do you have a paper cup?" Pamela asked.

I went to the bathroom and brought one back. Pamela went over the instructions again: "I'm supposed to pee in this cup, then put this dipstick in for five to ten seconds. . . ." She suddenly handed the instruction sheet to me. "I'm too nervous. You read it."

"'Immerse the dipstick in the collected urine for five to ten seconds,'" I read. "'A minute or two later you will see "pregnant" or "not pregnant" on the stick.'"

"I'll time it," said Liz, looking at her watch.

For fifteen seconds or so Pamela just sat on the bed holding the cup. But finally she squared her shoulders, took a deep breath, and went into the bathroom.

It seemed to be taking too long.

"Think we should go in there?" Liz asked.

Then we heard the door open and Pamela's footsteps in the hall. She was holding the half cup of urine, and she carefully placed it on my desk, a tissue beside it. "I'll do it in here," she said. "I want you guys to be with me."

She unwrapped the dipstick, then stuck it in the urine. "Count," she said.

"One . . . two . . . three . . . ," Liz began, looking again at her watch. At the count of ten Pamela took out the stick and laid it on the tissue. We gathered around.

"How long did it say, Alice?" Pamela asked.

I looked at the instructions again. "A minute or two."

I tried to remember when I had been this nervous, this uncomfortable, this terrified. We were staring at the dipstick as though it were some alien life-form that would suddenly start pulsating or breathing or beeping.

"It's starting to show," said Liz, and we all leaned forward as the letters became more visible.

And finally there it was. *Pregnant*, it read.

Pamela sat down on the bed again and cried.

I couldn't take my eyes off the stick. Maybe we had just missed it. Maybe the *not* was yet to come. But it didn't.

We sat down on either side of Pamela and let her cry. Babies were supposed to be happy occasions! How did this get so mixed up?

"H-he even said he'd marry m-me if it happened," Pamela wept.

Liz couldn't help herself. "But you guys are only *seventeen*!" she said.

Pamela violently shook her head. "I didn't want it to be like this. I don't want a guy marrying me because I'm pregnant. I'm not sure I even want to marry at all. I *know* I don't want this baby. And yet . . ." Her face screwed up again. "It . . . it's *T-Tim's!*"

We just sat there and stroked her hand. Her back.

When the tears stopped a second time, Pamela said, "Sometimes tests are wrong, you know! This could be a false positive. Maybe I should go back and buy a kit that just shows a plus or a minus. Or changes color or something. I mean, shouldn't you always get a second opinion?"

The doorbell rang and we all froze.

"It couldn't be Dad or Sylvia," I said. "Unless they lost their key." I stood up and went to the window. "It must be Gwen! It's her brother's car."

I was afraid that Pamela would tell me not to let her in, but Pamela just sat there on the bed like a wad of wet tissue, so I went downstairs and opened the door.

Gwen's good at reading faces. She just cocked her head and studied me. "I called Pamela's and no one answered," she said. "I called Liz's and her mom said she was over here. So I decided to drive Bill's car over and see what the heck is going on."

"Pamela's upstairs. Come on up," I told her.

As Gwen followed behind, she asked, "Is this something I'm not supposed to know?"

"Yeah," I said, and smiled a little over my shoulder. "Because you're too perfect and too smart to ever let this happen to you. But I think Pamela's accepting visitors now."

Gwen still looked puzzled. But when she entered my bedroom, she took it all in—the opened test kit on the floor, the cup of urine on my desk, the dipstick. And Pamela, forlorn and tearstained on the bed.

"Oh, girl!" Gwen said, and put an arm around her.

And then, Gwen the Practical took over. She pulled up the desk chair and sat facing Pamela.

"Okay, what's the plan?" she asked.

"Go to a convent, what else?" Pamela said grimly.

"Have you told Tim?"

"Yes. He knows I'm late. But he doesn't know this."

"What about your dad? Have you said anything to him or Meredith?"

"They'd kill me."

"Now listen, Pamela," said Gwen, taking her hand and gripping it hard. "You've got choices, you know. You don't have to decide anything right now. Got that? You don't even have to decide anything this week. Promise me—*promise me*—you won't do something stupid, like eat a whole box of Ex-Lax or jump off a roof or swallow a bottle of pills."

"I'm too tired to do anything but sleep," said Pamela.

"You *will* tell Tim, though, won't you? He needs to know."

"Yes."

"How did you get over here?"

"Walked. I just want to take a nap."

"Then c'mon, I'll drive you home," Gwen told her.

We all hugged Pamela, and then they left.

I looked at Liz. "I don't want Pamela there

by herself," I said. "I'm calling Tim."

When he answered—and *fortunately*, he answered—I said, "Pamela needs you, Tim. She's at home." And I didn't have to explain.

It was a rather somber seventeenth birthday for me the next day. I'd already told my family I didn't want a party, and I didn't. I was getting too old for a lot of fuss, and I was too wiped out worrying about Pamela to enjoy it much. I let Dad and Sylvia think I was just tired from studying for my finals.

I went to the newspaper staff meeting after school, and when I got home, Lester was there, and Sylvia was frosting the cake she'd baked the night before.

Lester blew on the little paper horn he'd stuck in one pocket, and I decided I was going to be cheerful no matter what. If I couldn't tell my family what the matter was, then I owed it to them not to play Guess Why I'm Grumpy.

"Looks delicious!" I told Sylvia of the German chocolate cake.

"Do you realize you were born in one of the most beautiful months of the year?" she said. "Just look at our yard. Everything that can bloom has blossomed."

"The flowers that bloom in the spring, tra la!" sang Lester, and even I recognized the song from *The Mikado*. The words, anyway.

What was really a surprise was that Dad came home bringing David, Marilyn, and her husband, Jack, along with him.

"Now, this isn't a party, Alice," Sylvia said quickly. "We just invited a few friends in for dinner."

I laughed and was grateful that there was *some* kind of a celebration after all—grateful for family. And I tried to keep Pamela out of my mind for the present.

Jack had brought his guitar, Marilyn brought flowers, and at seven sharp a delivery man from Levante's brought shish kebabs and tabbouleh and lemon rice soup. We had a feast.

"So this is the age when magical things happen, huh?" said Lester.

"Magical how?" asked Marilyn.

"Well, every time I pass a newsstand, I see that magazine, *Seventeen*. It's been in print forever, but it never says *Eighteen*. It's as though seventeen is the age a girl wants to be forever."

"Oh, no," said Marilyn. "Twenty-one. Definitely twenty-one."

"I say whatever age I am right now," said

Sylvia. "Whatever age I get to be, that's the best."

"Live in the moment," said David.

"So what's the magical age for a guy?" I asked Lester.

"Easy," he said. "The age he graduates."

"Amen to that," said Dad.

After dinner Jack played "Happy Birthday" for me on his guitar. Then he and Marilyn sang some duets they'd been performing at folk music concerts, their own arrangements. We'd had so much food that we sent some of it home with them when they left, and I gave them both a hug at the door.

I *really* appreciated my family that night. But of course the evening could not be complete without a phone call from Aunt Sally and Uncle Milt in Chicago.

"Happy birthday, honey," said Uncle Milt. "Wish we could be there to give you a hug."

"I wish you could too," I said, and thinking about his heart operation last fall, I asked, "How *are* you?"

"Fit as a fiddle," he said. "Taking good care of myself. But the big news here is that Carol is getting married in July to that Swenson boy. We like him a lot."

"Oh, we do too!" I said. "That's wonderful." And I told the others.

"Well, you'll all get invitations," said Aunt Sally on their speakerphone. "But I'm writing poetry now as my hobby, Alice, and I've composed a poem for your birthday. I mailed it to you with a card, but I'm afraid it won't get there until the weekend. So I'd like to read it to you."

"I can't wait to hear it," I said. "I'm going to hold the phone away from my ear so everyone can hear, Aunt Sally. Is that okay?"

"Of course!" she said. "And I'll speak louder." She cleared her throat and began:

> *When you were born a little girl,*
> *As pure as driven snow,*
> *We knew that you'd be tempted to*
> *Say 'yes' instead of 'no.'*

> *Your mother left our earthly home*
> *And asked me to take care*
> *That you would lead a virtuous life*
> *In thought and deed and prayer.*

> *We've watched you grow up straight*
> *and tall,*
> *So beautiful of face.*
> *And hoped that you would keep yourself*
> *In innocence and grace.*

But whether you are pure or not,
Or somewhere in between,
You'll always have our deepest love,
So, Happy Seventeen."

I hardly knew what to say. Aunt Sally has been worried about my virginity for almost as long as I can remember, but her preaching always comes at me sideways, and she thinks she's being subtle.

This time, though—maybe because I'm almost grown up—it didn't bother me a lot. I was moved that she cared for me so much, and I wished that Pamela had a mother she could talk to. Even an Aunt Sally.

"Thank you, Aunt Sally," I said. "It's an honor to have a poem composed just for me on my birthday."

After we'd talked a little about Carol's coming wedding and how the reception would be held in the hotel where the groom is manager, we said good-bye and I gently put down the phone.

"Only Aunt Sally!" Lester said, grinning. Turning to Dad, he asked, "Do you remember the article she sent me on my thirteenth birthday, warning me of the dangers of smoking? And the newspaper clipping on my eighteenth birthday about teenage drinking? Oh yeah. And the story

of the man who fathered eleven illegitimate children, and once they learned to trace DNA, they
tracked him down and made him pay eleven
mothers for child support? And Aunt Sally would
always write at the bottom of each article, 'But we
know this would never happen to you.'"

"What would we do without Sally?" Dad said.
"She got us through some rough times when
Marie died. Ah, yes. Sal and her poetry. Now, this
one's a keeper."

17

The Bus to Somewhere

I put on my pajamas at about ten thirty and was reading one more chapter in my sociology book when my phone rang. I glanced at the clock, puzzled, then reached down for my bag on the floor and took out my cell. Pamela.

"Pam?" I said, holding the phone to my ear.

"I feel horrible that I forgot your birthday," she said. Her nose sounded clogged.

"Hey, there's a lot on your mind," I said.

"How was it?"

"My birthday? Fun. Les came over, and Dad brought Marilyn and Jack and David from work. Jack played his guitar."

"What'd you get?"

"Money, mostly. Everybody's been asking what I wanted. My feet have grown a half size, I think, and I need new heels for the prom, among other things."

"Did Patrick give you anything?"

"A kiss. Before school."

"That's all?"

"It was a pretty good kiss."

"Who are you doubling with?"

"No one that I've heard. I think we're going alone."

"Uh-oh," said Pamela knowingly. Then, "I'm not keeping you from anything, am I?"

"Only sleep," I said. "Do you know what time it is?"

"Oh, I'm sorry," she said. But she didn't say good-bye. "Just wondering . . . do you and Sylvia have good talks? I mean, after that last quarrel over the car, can you tell her stuff?"

"Not entirely. Some. We're working on it."

"Lucky," said Pamela. And when she didn't say anything for so long that I started to ask about it, she interrupted and said, "Alice, I'm scared."

"I know you are," I told her. "How long are you going to keep this secret? You've got to talk with someone. An adult."

"Yeah? Like who?"

I couldn't tell if she was crying or not.

"I think you ought to tell your mom."

"Are you crazy?" she said. "Why would I listen to her?"

"She's still your mom."

"And hear her tell me all the mistakes *she's* made?"

"You'll have to take that chance," I said. "She didn't ask to be put in this position, remember. But you won't tell your dad or Meredith, and *someone's* got to know, Pamela. You need to start seeing a doctor."

She *was* crying now. "I don't *want* to go through this! I don't *want* this baby!"

"What does Tim want you to do?" I tried to be as gentle as I could.

"He said he's not ready to be a father, but he will if he has to. I don't want him to *have* to. I don't want *me* to have to. I just don't want to *be* in this mess!"

I thought of all the times Pamela had slept over—all the good times we'd had in my bedroom. The phone conversations. The laughter and jokes and music and movies and scrapbooks and bulletin boards and . . . We weren't even in college yet! How could Pamela be a mother? How would she act? What would she do?

We'd had this same conversation several times already. And each time Pamela said she didn't *want* to be pregnant, as though if she said it enough, it wouldn't happen. And the conversation always ended with Pamela in tears.

I think we were on the phone until around eleven thirty. My battery was going, and Pamela's voice was fading in and out. I told her we'd talk again the next day after school. We'd go somewhere and get ice cream, I said. Make a list of all the things she was worried most would happen, and we'd go over them one by one.

I dragged through the next morning. Probably no one except Gwen and Liz and Tim and I noticed that Pamela laughed too loud, sat too quiet, walked too fast, ate too slow. . . . It was as though none of these usual activities was familiar to her. Like she was playacting her life, trying to fit in, with a future so uncertain.

She fell asleep in sociology.

"Miss Jones, if you *please*?" the teacher said. "The musical's over now. . . ."

Tim, too, looked distracted, worried. How did a guy tell his parents that he was going to be a father? That eight months from now, he'd either be moving out to set up housekeeping or that a baby would be moving in? How did he ask his mom if she could babysit five days a week until the kid was in school? If he could bring a wife home to live in his bedroom? How did he give up plans for college and settle for bagging groceries at Giant? It wasn't just

Pamela and Tim whose lives would change; it was everyone's.

I was on my way to sixth period that afternoon when I saw Pamela, tears streaming down her face, walking rapidly toward the south exit.

"Pamela?" I called.

She kept going. There was something about her face that was frightening. I ran after her, ignoring the bell. She ran down the steps and out toward the soccer field.

"Pamela, stop!" I yelled again. "Wait up."

When I finally caught up with her, she was breathing in little gasps and spurts, and her eyes were so teary that she'd walked right into the fence.

I put my arms around her. "Talk to me," I said. "Tell me."

She kept crying. "Tim w-walked away," she said.

"When? What do you mean?"

"I w-was heading for his locker, and . . . I *know* he saw me! But he turned and walked away! Like he didn't even want to *talk* to me!"

I just held her. "Well, maybe he didn't want to talk right then. He's still trying to deal with all this too. And maybe he's mad at himself."

Pamela just sobbed into my shoulder. "Alice," she wept, "I w-want to call M-Mom."

• • •

By the time we got back to the street, she'd
changed her mind. I guided her into Ben & Jerry's
and bought her a dish of chocolate raspberry.

"Call her," I said.

"She won't be home," Pamela said. "She works
on Thursdays."

"Then we'll go over there when she gets
home."

Pamela took a bite of ice cream, then wiped
her eyes with her sleeve. "She's probably going
out tonight."

"You don't know that."

"I can guess."

"We'll call her at work," I said. I knew if we
didn't call right then, Pamela might not do it at
all. "Finish your ice cream, Pam, and then we'll
call."

She ate slowly, stirring the ice cream around
until it became soup.

"You know what she'll say," she said.

"No, and neither do you."

"She'll say, 'How did you get yourself in this
mess?'"

"And if she does?"

"I'll say, 'How did you get into the mess *you*
made for yourself?' And then we'll fight."

"Give me your cell phone, Pamela." She didn't

move, so I reached for her bag and retrieved it myself.

I knew that last period would be over soon, that kids would be leaving school. I'd been waiting for Pamela to finish her ice cream, but now I saw that she was crying again. Any minute crowds would be dropping by. The warm days of May were great for Ben & Jerry's.

"What's the number?" I asked Pamela, holding the cell phone out in front of me. "Do you have it programmed?"

She shook her head. "I don't know it."

I called information. "Nordstrom, Montgomery Mall, Bethesda, Maryland," I said. The operator gave me the number and connected me.

"What department?" I asked Pamela.

"Career wear," she said.

I repeated it into the phone, and when the extension started ringing, I handed the phone to Pamela.

Pamela waited until she heard her mother's greeting, and then, in a voice like a kitten's mew, she said, "Mom? I . . . I . . . I need to talk to you. Could I come over, m-maybe tonight?"

Please say she can come! I whispered in my head. *Please don't tell her you're going out.*

She must have been telling Pamela something, because Pam was quiet, listening. "All right, then," she said, and my heart sank. She ended the call and sat there staring at the cell in her hand, then at me.

"She's leaving for home. She said to come right over."

I think we had just missed a bus, because we waited twenty minutes for another. Then it was a twenty-five-minute ride to Glenmont Apartments.

Pamela's eyes were red, and she looked as though she hadn't slept for a while. I wondered if I should be coming along and told Pamela I could sit out on the steps or over in the kiddie playground while she and her mom talked. But Pamela said she wouldn't go inside unless I went with her.

"This is about the hardest thing I've ever had to do," she said. "You know what Dad would say if I told him I was pregnant? That I was growing up just like mom. What he'd mean is, a slut."

"He may have told you that once, Pamela, but has he said that recently?"

She thought about it. "No. I guess he's mellowed some since he met Meredith. But I don't think he's ever going to forgive Mom for walking out on us. I don't think he ever can."

"People change," I said.

"And sometimes for the worse."

"Sometimes."

Mrs. Jones must have gotten there just before we did, because she was still wearing heels and a silk top over her dark skirt. When she opened the door, she barely saw me at all. Just took one look at Pamela and opened her arms.

I sat in one corner of the living room, Pamela and her mom on the couch across from me. I think Mrs. Jones knew, even before Pamela opened her mouth, that she was pregnant.

"I . . . I'm going to have a baby, Mom," Pamela wept. "And I'm s-scared."

The grief on her mother's face turned to sympathy in moments. "Oh my God!" she breathed. "When, sweetheart?"

"I don't know. January, maybe."

Mrs. Jones was holding one of Pamela's hands in hers. "And . . . the father?"

"My boyfriend, Tim. He's a really nice guy, Mom. But I don't think he wants to be a father. . . ."

"Of course not." Mrs. Jones kept stroking the back of Pamela's hand. "Have you told your dad?"

"I'm not suicidal," Pamela said, making me smile a little.

"Or Meredith, either, I suppose. . . ."

"No."

"Oh God!" Mrs. Jones said again, shakily. She

pressed her lips tightly together, studying her daughter some more. "Are you sure about this?"

"Yeah. I took a test."

"How late are you?"

"Four weeks."

"But you haven't seen a doctor?"

"No."

Mrs. Jones nodded. "Do you want to keep it, Pamela? Have you thought about what you want to do?"

Want to keep it? The words chilled me. Imagining Pamela with a baby chilled me. How do you ever decide what's best for everybody?

"I don't *know*!" Pamela wept. "I don't want a baby, Mom, but . . . it's T-Tim's baby!"

"And yours," her mother said.

"What do *you* think I should do, Mom?"

"Pamela," said Mrs. Jones, "this is a decision you're going to have to make yourself, and it's one of the biggest decisions a woman could ever face." She didn't say *girl,* she said *woman.* "I don't think you should decide anything right this minute, but I want to take you to a doctor so we can talk about it and see what the choices are."

I sat silently through the long conversation. Mrs. Jones was saying all the right things, it seemed—that whatever Pamela decided to do about the baby, she'd support her. That Pamela hadn't ruined her life—she had to believe that—but she was taking a detour. And that somehow they would get through this together. She told Pamela that they would get all the information they could about her choices—abortion, keeping the baby, or giving it up for adoption—that it was a situation none of them wanted to be in, but they were. People made mistakes in their lives, and this was a big one. But she knew what it was like to make a mistake.

I excused myself to go to the bathroom, then purposely stalled to give them some time alone. I'd taken my bag and cell phone with me, and I tried to call Sylvia to tell her I'd be late for dinner, but I hadn't recharged the battery and couldn't get through.

When I finally went back in the living room, Pamela was standing by the door, hugging her mom. And as we left, Mrs. Jones said, "Thank you for coming, Alice," and hugged me, too. Her eyes were so sad.

Pamela was quiet on the way back to the bus stop. She looked drained. Relieved, maybe, but sad. Everything about this was sad. But just before the bus came, she leaned against me, hugging my arm, and said, "Thank you, Alice. I'm glad I talked with Mom. I'm glad you made me do it."

"I didn't make you. Encouraged you, maybe," I told her. "But I'm glad you gave her the chance to act like a mother."

We got on board and took a seat near the back. "It's good that it's almost summer," Pamela said. "I won't have to answer a lot of questions at school if I've got morning sickness. Maybe I'll go live at Mom's after I start to show. For a while, anyway. First, I guess, I have to decide if I'm going to keep the baby."

"And you have time to think about it, Pamela," I said, and glanced over at her. "You won't do anything impulsive, will you?"

"Like a clothes hanger, you mean?"

"Like *any*thing that isn't safe."

"I won't," she promised.

I could have gotten a transfer to another bus that would have taken me to Georgia Avenue, but I was tense and needed to walk off some anxiety. So I said good-bye to Pamela and got off at a corner where I had seven blocks yet to go. After a while, I thought, you have to stop telling yourself that it can't be happening and realize that it can. That it is. And that somebody you've known since sixth grade, someone you love, is an expectant mom and has to deal with it.

I was a block from home when I realized it was almost seven, and I still hadn't called Sylvia.

I could hardly believe it was so late! I should have used Pam's cell.

When I got in the house, I called, "I'm home! Sorry I'm late."

I could smell Sylvia's homemade spaghetti sauce. Dad's special garlic bread.

"We put some dinner aside for you, Alice. Help yourself," Sylvia called from the family room.

I was glad I could eat alone and would do it later, because I wasn't hungry. I went upstairs and dropped my bag on the rug, realizing that I'd left not only my sweater at school, but my books, my homework, my assignments. . . . Suddenly I felt exhausted. I lay down on my bed and closed my eyes, one arm across my forehead.

I'd probably been there about ten minutes when there was a light tap on the door.

"Al?" Dad said. "Can I come in?"

"Sure," I said, but didn't get up.

He stood looking at me a minute, then pulled a chair over. I could barely see his face from where I was laying, but I still felt too tired to get up.

"Anything wrong?" he asked.

"I'm okay," I said, begging the question.

"When Sylvia got home, she checked the voice messages," Dad said. "There was an automated call from the attendance office saying that you skipped sixth period."

Damn! I thought. Why did they have to be so darn efficient? Skip a class, it's transmitted immediately to the school office, and the phone call gets made.

"What was that all about?" Dad asked.

"Something really important came up," I said. "There was something I had to do, that's all."

Silence. I hate silence almost more than anything. More than quarreling.

"I'm worried about you," Dad said finally. "Is there anything you want to tell me?"

"No. Why are you worried?"

"Because . . . I was emptying the wastebaskets before dinner—for the trash pickup tomorrow—and I found this."

I looked over and saw that he was holding something in one hand, and I sat up. There was the wrapper from the pregnancy test kit.

"It's not mine," I said quickly, which sounded totally ridiculous, because it had been in *my* wastebasket.

"Al," Dad said. "All these years I've tried to keep an open relationship with you and Les. And I know that at seventeen you tell me only a small percentage of what goes on in your life, and that's only natural. I don't have to know everything. But when it's something serious, I hope you'll tell me."

"I will," I said. "But I wasn't the one who took that test, Dad. I can't tell you more than that. Not yet. But I'm sorry that it got you worried about me. Really."

Dad was so relieved that I could see the crease lines disappearing on his forehead, the little smile crinkles at the corners of his eyes growing deeper.

"Okay, honey. I won't ask. Except . . . where were you this afternoon? Can you at least tell me that?"

I smiled a little. "We weren't doing anything illegal or dangerous. Just having a talk with somebody's mom."

He didn't say anything. Just sat there smiling at me. Finally he said, "Did I ever tell you I think you're great?"

I smiled a little too. "I don't remember those exact words."

"I never said you were fantastic?"

"Nope. Not that, either."

He was grinning now. "Trustworthy, loyal, helpful, friendly, courteous, kind . . . ?"

"Keep talking," I said.

"Come on down and I'll heat up that garlic bread for you," he told me, and I followed him downstairs.

18

Finale

I hadn't asked Patrick for the details of prom night, because that kind of thing bores him. He isn't much for stuff like clothes and flowers and photos and such. But it was *his* senior prom, *his* invitation, so I would go along with whatever he had planned. Or hadn't planned. All he'd told me was that he'd pick me up at six and to bring a change of clothes for the after-prom party at school. But I'd go with Patrick if he wore a Hawaiian shirt and rode up to our house on a bicycle.

Because Marilyn had loaned me a dress and Dad and Sylvia didn't need to help me buy a new one, Sylvia said she'd pay for my hair appointment—I wanted it piled high on top of my head, with curls in back. Then Dad said he'd pay for a manicure, which was their way of telling me they were glad that Patrick was back in the picture and that I wasn't going out with guys like Tony.

"Hey," I told them, "you'd think I was getting married or something."

But I really did want to look different for Patrick's prom. Blend in with the seniors. I wanted to look older, mysterious. Seductive, even. I hate fake nails, though—hate what they do to your natural ones—and only a professional manicurist could make my old nails look glamorous.

Liz came over to give me a pedicure. The guys she'd dated this semester were all juniors, so she hadn't been invited to the prom. But she knew I'd be wearing my new beige strappy sandals and wanted to make sure that my toes were gorgeous.

"Patrick doesn't notice toes," I said, but willingly rested one foot in her lap.

"How do you know?" She massaged lotion into my heels. "He could have a secret fetish and go nuts over women's shoes. But frankly, I think he's more of a butt man."

My eyes opened wide. "A *what*?"

"Hey. Men are divided into three groups, you know: breasts, legs, and butts. And I've seen Patrick's eyes following you out of a room, so I think he's a butt guy."

I laughed. "Those are all brain-dead guys,

Liz. Isn't there a category for guys who take in the whole girl?"

"I'm still looking," she said.

I loved the Burnished Copper color the manicurist had used on my nails, so I'd bought a bottle of it, and now Liz was using it on my toenails.

"Remember when Pamela painted—," she said, and then stopped. I think we were both remembering the time in eighth grade when Pamela had inked J-U-I-C-Y on each foot—one letter on each toenail—and the gym teacher gave her polish remover and made her take it off.

I figured that Liz didn't want to ruin my evening by bringing up Pamela, so that's why she didn't finish the sentence. But I don't think either of us could stop thinking about her, not really.

"Sorry," Liz said. "I didn't mean to remind you of that."

"She's on our minds no matter what," I said.

Liz sighed and carefully brushed Dry Kwik over the polish of each toenail. "And it will never be like we planned, will it? I mean, we'll never go to the same college or drive to California like we wanted. Everything changes in the blink of an eye."

"That's life, I guess," I told her. "Or, as David would say, that's what makes life so 'terrifyingly wonderful.'"

We did my makeup last. I'd bought a bronze blush with glitter in it, and after I did my foundation and powder, Liz did my brows, my mascara, and my eyeliner, then topped it off with the bronze blush on my cheekbones.

We'd told Sylvia we'd invite her up for a final inspection, but I didn't want to put on my heels till I had to; I'd be on my feet all evening as it was. Forty minutes before Patrick was to pick me up, my cell phone rang.

Liz and I looked at each other.

"If Patrick tells you he can't make it, tell him you'll never speak to him again, *ever*!" Liz said. "Remember how he got mono the night of the eighth-grade semi-formal?"

"As though it was his fault!" I said, reaching for the phone. But it wasn't Patrick's number. "It's Pamela," I told Liz.

We both stared at the phone. I was afraid to answer. What if Pamela was crying? What if she was threatening to do something awful? What if she really, desperately needed to see me again? What if . . . ?

"Should I answer for you? Tell her you're just about ready to leave? That you've left?" Liz asked.

I shook my head and picked up my cell.

Pamela was breathless. Again. I couldn't tell

if she'd been crying or not. "Listen, Alice, I know you're getting ready for prom, and I didn't want to upset you and I'll only take a minute and you don't have to come over, but . . . I don't think I'm pregnant anymore."

"*What?*" I cried, and Liz looked stricken.

"About an hour ago I felt like I had to go, and I went to the toilet and passed these really big clumps of blood. I was cramping and there was blood in the toilet, and I think . . . I think everything came out."

I didn't know what to say.

"Could you . . . could you tell . . . by looking?" I asked finally.

"Just big clumps of blood."

"But . . . are you *okay?*"

Liz was trying to read my face, and I made a sweeping motion between my legs. She understood and sat with her lips apart, waiting.

"I called Mom," Pamela said, "and she called her gynecologist, and he said if I wasn't cramping anymore and the bleeding had stopped, it was probably a complete miscarriage."

"Oh, Pamela!" I said. "I'm . . . I'm . . ."

"Glad," she answered for me.

"You didn't . . . ?"

"No. No coat hangers or Ex-Lax or jumping or anything. Mom said that somehow I lucked out, but I couldn't count on that ever happening again. The doctor wants to see me tomorrow, and we've got an appointment at the clinic. If I start bleeding or cramping again, Mom will take me to the emergency room."

I was doubtful. "You're not just making up this story so I'll have a good time tonight and won't worry about you?"

"Honest. I called Tim before I called you, and you know what he said? He said that the last couple of weeks have been the worst of his life. I told him, me too. But listen, have a great time, okay?"

"Are you alone now?" I asked.

"Yeah. Meredith's out somewhere, and Dad's watching a baseball game. He doesn't have a clue. Mom's coming over later to get me. I'm going to spend the night with her."

Liz was motioning to herself, then pointing in the direction of Pamela's house. "Do you want Liz to come over? She just gave me a pedicure," I said.

"Oh no, Alice! She's there to help on your big night!"

"Hey. She's volunteering." I handed the phone to Liz.

"Pamela," she said, "I'm through here. And I'll be right over." She handed the phone back to me.

"Alice?" said Pamela. And now her voice

sounded choked. "You're the best, you know it?"

"And you're the bravest," I told her.

I ended the call, and Liz said, "She had a miscarriage, right?"

"Yeah, and we're celebrating. It's weird, isn't it? If she was married and wanting a baby, we'd all be in tears. Her mom said to consider herself lucky but not to count on it happening again."

"Oh, man! It'll be nice having the old Pamela back, won't it?" Liz said, gathering up her bag.

"You can't go through something like this and not be changed a little," I said. "And maybe that's a good thing."

Patrick didn't come in a limo, and he didn't come in his dad's car. He and fifteen other couples came in an old school bus they had hired for the evening, with a big banner stretched along one side reading PROM OR BUST. All the windows were dropped down, and as soon as I opened our front door, we could hear all the laughing and chatter coming from inside it.

"Wow!" I said, partly for the bus, partly for Patrick, who was dressed in a white tuxedo, white vest, and white tie, a handsome contrast to his face, still lightly tanned from his week of landscaping work during spring break. "Patrick, you look terrific!"

"And you're gorgeous," he said, kissing me lightly on the lips when he handed me a wrist corsage of white baby roses, tied with an aqua ribbon. He must have called Sylvia at some point about my dress.

I put a boutonniere in his lapel, and we posed for pictures for Dad and Sylvia in front of the stone fireplace in our family room. They even got a picture of us on the porch, with the bus in the background.

Then we were climbing aboard with my after-prom bag under a seat, and Patrick introduced me to some of the other seniors. I didn't really know any of them. I'm sure I'd seen them around school, but it's hard to recognize people who are all dressed up in glitter and tulle and fancy tuxedos with bow ties.

The ones Patrick knew best were a Latino couple, Mario and Ana, and his Asian friend, Ron Yen, and his date, Melinda. One of the many things you can say for Patrick is that he's international, and he speaks four languages. But if I ever thought that Patrick was all work and no play, that he didn't know how to have fun, prom proved me wrong.

The bus took us to Clyde's, where we sat at long tables, guys across from their dates, and we feasted on crab cakes and steak and chocolate mousse. Ron and Mario kept us laughing, telling how they had asked their dates to prom. Mario said he printed the question on a big sheet of poster board and planted it in Ana's front yard. Great idea, he said, except that her dad came out and told him to stay off the lawn, he'd just planted grass seed, and to bring the sign inside.

"So here I am, walking in their living room, holding this huge sign on a stick, and I knocked a picture off the wall," said Mario.

Then Ron said he'd been thinking for weeks of a creative way to ask Melinda to go with him, and finally he invited her out to dinner and persuaded the waiter to bring her a piece of cake with *Prom?* written in frosting. But either the waiter couldn't spell or the *o* looked like an *a,* because it came to the table reading *Pram?*

And Melinda said, "I looked at it and said, 'Pram? A baby carriage? What is this, a proposal or a proposition?'" We shrieked with laughter.

No one asked if Patrick had invited me in some creative way; he had simply phoned and asked. But I'll bet none of the other girls had been asked five months in advance, on New Year's Day. Patrick and I just smiled at each other across the table.

• • •

We got to the prom at the Holiday Inn about nine and took our bags in with us so we could change in the restrooms later. The ballroom ceiling was dark, studded with pinpoints of light, as though we were dancing outside under the stars. Potted plants along the sides of the room gave the feel of an island veranda, and as we passed a mirrored wall, I caught a glimpse of my face and my hair— Marilyn's dress with its satin-trimmed layers— and I looked good. No, I looked great. My dress was different from all the other dresses—very elegant and sophisticated and chic.

I didn't *feel* especially chic or sophisticated or elegant—just good. Just me. Like I was *almost* comfortable with who I was right then. I liked Patrick's friends. I liked the way he *made* friends— the way he could be different and still be funny, be smart, be Patrick.

"Hey, babe," he said, putting his hands on my waist and moving me out onto the dance floor.

"Hey, guy," I said, and put my head against his chest as we slow-danced along the edge of the ballroom.

I was having a wonderful time, and yet not a single one of my close friends—other than Patrick—was here. I could be part of the senior crowd and no one looked at me as though I didn't belong. I caught a glimpse of Don and Christy having their picture taken, and we danced by Scott and his date. I just smiled in his direction as Patrick turned me around and we moved on across the floor.

At some point in the evening, when I went out on a balcony with Patrick, I *almost* told him that Pamela had miscarried. Then I caught myself, realizing it was Pamela's secret—or story—to tell, not mine. Another one of those things you just "hold in your heart," as they say, and learn to keep to yourself.

So I just stood on the balcony with Patrick, my arms around his neck, the breeze in my hair.

"You surprise me, Patrick," I said after we'd kissed. "You look so good tonight. I mean, I figured you as a black tuxedo man, if you wore a tux at all."

"Symbol of my purity." He grinned.

When the couple who had been occupying the one bench went inside, Patrick and I took it over. He had his arm around me and pulled me closer.

"Having a good time?" he asked.

"Yes," I said. "I like watching you enjoy yourself. You usually seem so . . . so busy. Like you're running your life on a railroad timetable or something."

"That's not a compliment, right?"

"Just an observation. I like to see you having

fun. Sometimes you seem so driven. Do you ever feel that way? Driven?"

He appeared to be thinking it over. "Just the way I'm wired, I guess. Only child syndrome, I suppose."

"Your parents push you, you mean?"

"No. They've never really pushed me at all. But then, no brothers or sisters to compete with, so . . . I don't know. I've always looked up to Dad—being a diplomat, the diplomatic license plate and all . . . the dinners, the parties—and Mom used to be a college administrator . . . Ph.D. When there's just the three of you, you don't want to be the only flunky."

"Flunky! Patrick, you're good at *everything*!"

"No way."

"Name one thing you're not good at."

"Uh . . . let's see." I could tell by his voice that he was smiling. "Conversation?"

"You could talk the wind out of the whole debate team."

"Clothes? Style?"

"No complaints there."

"Well, let's see. Kissing?"

"You *could* use more practice," I said.

He cupped one hand under my chin, turned my face around, and we kissed, both of us smiling.

Then he backed away a little and looked down at me, and this time his face was serious. For several seconds he just studied me, like his eyes were conversing with mine. And then he leaned slowly toward me, kissed me lightly on the lips, and then he gave me a full, forceful kiss that almost sucked the breath out of me. After that he just held me close, my lips against his neck, and I drank in that wonderful, familiar Patrick scent.

We went back inside as other couples came out to get away from the music for a while. Teachers must hate prom duty. At the beginning of the evening they're all smiles and compliments, joking around with us, telling us how great we look. But by eleven thirty or so, you can tell they're waiting for that last slow dance of the evening, signaling that the end is in sight, so that they can get home and go to bed.

But for us, the night was still young. We were waiting for midnight too, and soon the restrooms were filled with girls exchanging their satin slip dresses and their lavender tulle for jeans and shorts and T's.

We filed back out to the bus, our dresses thrown over our arms, our strappy heels, strapless bras, dangly earrings, and wrist corsages tucked away in our travel bags. When we reached the school gym, we piled out and got in line at the door for the post-prom party.

I'd never been to one before, but I'd heard kids talk about those parties as even more fun than the prom. And though all the work was done by parents—it was *run* by parents—it was definitely *the* place to go from one until six in the morning.

The parties change from year to year, but we walked into the school to find that the hallway had been transformed into a Wild West set, and we felt as though we were walking down an unpaved street, with saloons and bawdy houses and cigar stores and saddle shops on either side of us. From a hidden speaker, a honky-tonk piano played a ragtime tune, and there was laughter and raucous talk in the background.

"Wow!" said Patrick, handsome now in jeans and a T-shirt. We didn't know what to try first, so we followed Ron and Melinda along a huge obstacle course that took us up close to the ceiling of the basketball court—through tunnels, across bridges, climbing over nets and going down slides.

When we came down to floor level again, Ron and Melinda went off to rock climb while Mario and Ana and Patrick and I went to the "casino" to play the roulette wheel, using fake money. I stopped and stared, because there at the next table, the blackjack table, was Mr. Long! Patrick's dad! The redheaded man with graying hair and the trim mustache! The diplomat! Dealing blackjack! He pretended not to know us, but he was hiding a smile.

Patrick laughed.

"I knew they were helping out, but I didn't know how," he said.

"You mean your mom's here too?" I asked, and then there she was. The slim, elegant woman—the Ph.D., the college administrator—in a Western shirt and jeans, pouring drinks (sparkling cider) at the saloon.

"Hi, Alice!" she called, and made a point of not acting like Patrick's mom, for which I'm sure he was grateful.

We walked along "streets" lined with cowboy boots and cactus ornaments, our feet crunching on peanut shells, craning our necks to see what the crowd was watching at one end of the gym. Then we howled at the sight of Mario and another guy slipping into enormous padded sumo wrestling bodysuits and helmets covered with fake sumo-style hair. Outfitted with the mock fat of four-hundred-pound wrestlers, the two of them crashed their stuffed bellies into each other until one of them fell over.

Then we had to try the game where we were blindfolded one by one and ushered into a tent with see-through vinyl sides. There we tried to grab one-dollar bills and gift certificates that were swirling about in the air.

"Alice," said Ana, grabbing my arm, "you gotta try this with me." And with the guys looking on, she dragged me over to these crazy oversized toilet bowls that went whizzing around a track. I don't know what they had to do with a Western theme, but like providing sumo wrestlers, parents try to squeeze in every possible gimmick they think would appeal to us. I gamely climbed on one, Ana on the other, and someone pressed the starter button.

With kids cheering us on, the motorized toilet bowls raced around in a circle, but at some point I fell in—no water, of course—and I couldn't get out while the bowl was moving. With only my arms and legs dangling over the sides, the toilet bowl continued to whiz, with everyone shrieking and clapping. When they finally pulled me out, Patrick was laughing so hard, he was doubled over. Somebody even took a picture.

It was silly, it was meaningless, and it was about the most fun I'd ever had in my life. I couldn't wait to tell my friends about it. Couldn't wait to see Pamela's face—relaxed, for a change—and hear her funny laugh.

But I especially wanted to tell them how Patrick looked riding the mechanical bull, thighs gripping the leather, and how—one hand clutching the cord, the other hand in the air—he held on for twenty-two seconds, beating the night's record. Who would have thought?

Students weren't allowed to come back to the party once they left, but there were places we could go when we needed a break. So about four o'clock, with country music playing, Patrick and I sat down on the floor at one end of the gym, our backs against a dune made of sandbags, and shared a Coke.

Patrick's legs were sprawled out in front of him, and he leaned against my shoulder, one hand on my leg. I caressed his arm and nuzzled the top of his head.

"Patrick," I asked, "when do you leave for the U?"

"Three weeks," he murmured.

"Three *weeks*?" I said.

"Classes start in June," he reminded me.

"I'm going to miss you," I sighed. Somehow I thought we'd have more time.

"I'll miss *you*," he said.

"What, exactly?" I asked. "Tell me what you'll

miss the most. My sultry smile? My bedroom eyes? My legs? My backside? *What?*"

"Hmmm," Patrick said sleepily. "You've got a great shoulder, you know."

"Shoulder?"

"To lean on."

I tipped back my head and smiled. I sort of liked that. I guess I *did*. And maybe it was enough.

"Yeah," I said. "Maybe I do."